"W_____" Holly _____.

He was too stunned to reply immediately.

"Do you want me to get all decked out in silk and go to fancy restaurants with you? I'll do that. Do you want me to stand around at elegant cocktail parties and pretend to be brainless and beautiful? I can do that too. Or would you like me to stay home and rub your feet and cook your meals and wash your clothes? Well, I can do that, too, but not all the time. I have a life, Oliver, and I want you to be part of it. I want to be part of your life, too, but I won't choose one life over another."

"I won't ask you to," he said, accepting the truth of her words. It was all or nothing with Holly, and that included her work at the clinic. "I'm not even sure I'd want you to. I don't always like what you do, but I respect and admire it. Can't I be proud of you and worry about you at the same time?"

"Yes, but—"

"I want time, Holly." He took a step closer. "Not messages. Not calls on phone machines. Real time. With you. I'll take what I can get . . . but I'll get what I can take too." His mouth closed hard and fast over hers, a shattering contrast to the soft, slow sweep of his tongue as he cinched her in his arms. . . .

WHAT ARE *LOVESWEPT* ROMANCES?

They are stories of true romance and touching emotion. We believe those two very important ingredients are constants in our highly sensual and very believable stories in the LOVE-SWEPT line. Our goal is to give you, the reader, stories of consistently high quality that may sometimes make you laugh, sometimes make you cry, but are always fresh and creative and contain many delightful surprises within their pages.

Most romance fans read an enormous number of books. Those they truly love, they keep. Others may be traded with friends and soon forgotten. We hope that each LOVESWEPT romance will be a treasure—a "keeper." We will always try to publish

LOVE STORIES YOU'LL NEVER FORGET
BY AUTHORS YOU'LL ALWAYS REMEMBER

The Editors

WAIT FOR ME

MARY KAY McCOMAS

BANTAM BOOKS
NEW YORK · TORONTO · LONDON · SYDNEY · AUCKLAND

WAIT FOR ME

A Bantam Book / August 1994

Bantam Books are published by Bantam Books, a division of Bantam Dou-
bleday Dell Publishing Group, Inc. Its trademark, consisting of the words
"Bantam Books" and the portrayal of a rooster, is Registered in U.S. Patent
and Trademark Office and in other countries. Marca Registrada. Bantam
Books, 1540 Broadway, New York, New York 10036.

PRINTED IN THE UNITED STATES OF AMERICA

OPM   0 9 8 7 6 5 4 3 2 1

Sometimes I'm hot and
sometimes I'm not
—oh well.
Yet she's always soft-spoken and tactful
—as hell.

So after fifteen stories,
It's time to share the glories,
I send my thanks daily
To my editor, Susann Brailey.

PROLOGUE

On October sixteenth Holly Ann Loftin died.

She wasn't sure how it happened. She didn't know why. It occurred quickly, unexpectedly, and she didn't linger to ascertain the details. They didn't matter . . . nothing did.

That was, perhaps, the most surprising part of dying. Nothing mattered. She didn't mind dying. It was a bit of relief to have it over with, to shed her body and go on.

There was, however, a brief period of adjustment that seemed rather peculiar. Familiar, too, as if she'd done it before, many times.

With the sloughing of earthly weight, worries, and wrongs, came the perfect peace and contentment her temporal being had instinctively sought since birth. Never able to define it or gather all its ingredients into one pot, it came to her as something she'd always known.

She knew the light as well. Brilliant. Brightest of all light. Bold. Intrinsic. Welcoming. If she'd had to compare it to anything, it might have been to going home or returning to a happy childhood or revisiting one's happiest moments on earth . . . only better. It gently pulled at her, drawing her in as one might softly draw in a breath of fresh air. And she went willingly, joyfully.

She was isolated in the light, but not alone. It was as if she were a brightly lit molecule of air in space, with zillions of other brightly lit molecules that she could neither see nor feel. But she could sense their presence, their energy, their oneness with the whole. And she was a part of it, always had been, always would be.

She was profoundly and boundlessly happy. Even as she felt the joining with another, the joy and serenity were limitless.

"You are premature."

"I belong here with you."

"We are always together."

"I couldn't find you."

"You are premature. Our time has yet to be."

"Here our time is always."

"Here. There. Our love changes not."

She reveled in the truth, exultant.

"You are premature. You must return."

"No. You are here."

"Only that part of me which dwells eternally within your soul is here. Go back. Wait for me."

"I did wait. I was lonely. I was lost. I needed you."

"Go back. Wait for me."

That part of the bright light which was her, began to fade.

"I belong here."

"Wait for me."

"How will I know you this time?"

"My heart will speak to yours as always. Time will stop and the earth shall tremble beneath us. In your great wisdom you will know me as no other. Your eyes shall reflect my love for you, and I will know you as before."

"You won't try to have me burned as a witch again, will you?" She sensed enjoyment, something akin to humor, and amplified it in her consciousness. "Or have me sent into slavery? Or mark me as an outcast to the tribe again? As a mortal, you are not always as malleable as you might be."

"And you are not always judicious."

"I am always eager to be with you."

"And I with you. Go back. Wait for me."

The light in her dimmed further.

"Hurry."

"Wait for me."

ONE

She couldn't help but notice his pain. The emptiness in his dark eyes was heartrending. They were red rimmed, too, though she suspected it was not from shedding tears as much as from a constant battle to keep them at bay.

The flight from San Francisco to Los Angeles wasn't long, but because she was pressed between a very large woman on her left and a grieving man on her right, the trip was taking on interminable dimensions.

Not that she was complaining, mind you. She had only to look at the poor sad man in the window seat, who appeared to be rather tall, to know that he was far more cramped than she. It was just that . . . well, she was afraid that her right leg had gone to sleep.

She tried to shift her position and bumped the lady's elbow, jarring the book in her pudgy hand. The woman sighed, loudly.

The tiny bit of circulation she'd restored to her leg made it begin to tingle with life. She tensed and relaxed her leg muscles, but it didn't help. Soon the tingling was like an electric shock, giving her leg a life of its own. It shook like a dog's at a fire hydrant.

The man looked at her leg, then raised his sorrowful gaze to her face.

"Sorry," she muttered.

He was a handsome man in spite of his unhappiness. Thick dark hair. Stalwart features. A strong jaw. She wondered briefly what he might look like when he was happy—if he was ever happy.

He went back to staring out the window.

Holly sighed quietly. There didn't seem to be enough air to get a full breath. She sighed again. It was better the second time. But the plane was getting hotter and stuffier by the minute. Or maybe she was bored and needed to think about something else.

She did a quick mental scan of her Christmas list and then composed another index of to-dos while she was in Los Angeles.

No, she decided, a few minutes later, she wasn't bored. It was definitely getting stuffy. If she could reach the little air nozzle above her . . .

Slowly she raised the arm that the woman wasn't lying on. She couldn't reach the nozzle without sitting up straight—and that would disturb both of her traveling companions. Discouraged, she lowered her arm and hit the man square in the chest.

His look was one of surprise. As if he'd just that moment realized she was there.

"Sorry."

He went back to staring out the window.

How long had they been in the air? she wondered. An hour? Two hours? She tried to sneak a peek out the man's window, to see if they were circling the airport. She moved into his peripheral field of vision, and he turned his head to look at her. Their noses bumped.

"Sorry," she said, grimacing. When her need to know overwhelmed her reluctance to disturb him, she blurted out, "What time is it?"

He looked at his watch. He frowned, tapped the crystal several times, then muttered a curse.

"My watch stopped," he said, turning back to the window.

"Is this the longest flight from San Francisco to L.A. you've ever been on, or what? I feel like I've been here for days," she said to no one particular, simply needing to speak.

The woman beside her turned a page in her book. The man shifted his legs uncomfortably and tried to ignore her.

"You must feel like you've been here for weeks," she said, and when he looked at her, she added, "You look real uncomfortable, wadded up in your seat that way. Time always seems a lot slower when you're uncomfortable . . . and when you're in a hurry."

"What makes you think I'm in a hurry?" He was watching her the way he might a bug he couldn't reach with his shoe or swat at with a newspaper.

"If you weren't in a hurry, you'd have booked your flight earlier and gotten a better seat—on the aisle or in first class," she said, noting the fine cloth and superior fit of his suit. Then, despite her best intentions, she said, "I hope it's nothing too serious. I hope everything turns out for the best."

"You hope what's not too serious?"

"The unhappiness you're going to face in L.A."

He scowled at her as if she were just another California nut dressed in human's clothing, and turned back to the window.

She sat silently, pinched between her mute travel mates, until the flight attendant stopped her cart beside them. She wasn't thirsty, but she ordered and paid for a little bottle of Jack Daniels and refused the ice. The flight attendant moved on.

Holly stared mindlessly at the tiny bottle and empty cup for several minutes before she twisted the top off and poured the brown liquid smoothly into the plastic cup. She handed it to the man.

A soft nudge to his leg drew his attention to her gift. His gaze lifted to her face, shifted over the seat to see that the attendant had passed by without his notice, then returned to the woman beside him.

Her eyes were golden brown, he observed, taking the cup from her fingers spontaneously. Nice hands, long and well groomed. But her eyes . . . Why hadn't he noticed before how rich they were? How they seemed to look straight into him?

And the cup? One whiff told him it was whiskey. It triggered a deep, familiar reflex in his brain, telling him it would dull his pain a bit. Like a trusting patient, frightened and reckless in his need for relief, he gulped the potion down.

"Thanks," he said, the whiskey still hot and burning in his throat, the calm reassurance in her eyes intensifying the warmth in his belly. He handed the cup back to her, noting the Jack Daniels label on the bottle. His brand. "Let me pay you."

He started to squirm in his seat, reaching into his breast pocket for his wallet. Her hand covered his through the cloth. His gaze lifted to hers. His heart pounded against his hand.

She shook her head once and removed her hand. Without words, she told him that to repay her act of kindness would be a huge insult. He wasn't in the mood and he didn't have the energy to insult anyone, much less this strange woman with the heart-shaped face and the earth-colored eyes, as warm and wise as the land itself.

He nodded his thanks once more, then turned back to the window.

Holly sat for long moments wondering why she'd bought the man a drink. She was glad she had, but . . . well, she hadn't thought about it. She'd just done it mindlessly, the way she would scratch an itch on the end of her nose.

It was strange indeed, but she wasn't one to over-analyze things. There didn't seem to be much point in it when everything in her life was strange to one degree or another anyway.

While the engines hummed, her thoughts grew heavy, and she was warm in the close quarters. She became drowsy and closed her eyes.

"My father's dying," the man said out of the blue. Holly opened her eyes. She turned her head to look at him. He was still facing the window. "Heart attack. It's not his first."

Instinctively Holly curled her fingers over the hand on his leg. It jerked away, then quickly returned to snatch her hand into a tight grasp.

It was an odd moment. They didn't speak, and he

didn't look away from the window. There was a tension between them, the kind any two strangers holding hands would experience. But underneath the tension something special happened. Something as basic as being human. Something often overlooked and trampled upon in the normal hustle and bustle of life.

Suffering met with compassion.

The Fasten Seat Belt light blinked on and still they sat, needing and comforting without words. It wasn't until the plane began its descent that he loosened his hold and let her hand slip away.

He looked at her then, feeling self-conscious and stupid. He was heartsick about his father, but it wasn't as if his dad's impending death hadn't been expected. On every visit over the past year, his father had been weaker and more frail. The reality of losing him was painful, certainly, but to turn to a complete stranger for sympathy? It was very out of character for him.

"Do you live in L.A., or are you visiting?" he asked, hiding behind a little small talk.

"Visiting. For the holiday."

"That's right. Thanksgiving. I forgot," he said. "You have family here?"

She laughed. It was a soft, joyous noise that made him smile.

"I have family everywhere, all over the place."

"That must be nice. I'm an only child."

"Then losing your father is especially terrible for you. I'm sorry."

"Thanks. And . . . thanks for before too," he said, looking all around the cabin, but not at her.

He caught himself. Why not look at her? He turned

his head and did exactly that. She was easy to look at. She had a nice face. Not beautiful, but very nice, with smooth, creamy skin and almond-shaped eyes that tilted upward a bit. She was wearing one of those simple floral-print dresses that reminded him of another time, a more graceful era in history. Her hair was almost as dark as his own, though the overhead light showed red highlights in the deep hues of mahogany. And then there was her mouth.

Her mouth was especially nice. It looked soft and warm and giving . . . a lot like the woman herself, now that he thought about it. Those three words could have been stamped on her forehead. She wasn't a heart stopper, but there was a softness and warmth about her, a nurturing quality like a young mother's.

"Do you have children?" she asked, jarring him a bit, as if she'd taken her question from his thoughts.

"No. Why?"

"Family is a good thing to have. Children could be a comfort to you now."

"You think so?"

"No. Not really. I don't have anything against children, but I don't think they'd make you feel any better about losing your father. I don't think anything could."

"Then why did you say that children could be a comfort to me now?"

"Because they could be. I mean, it is possible. People say they are. But I don't have any, so I don't know. I just don't think it's likely."

"Uh-huh." He didn't know what else to say.

"Are you married, at least?" she asked, worried about him.

"No."

"You're not?" She was amazed and it showed. It made him smile a little.

"Never even come close," he said to add to the effect. Truth be known, it amazed him. He wanted a wife and children, but it was always a someday thing, something that would happen when he got the signal—maybe if he were struck by lightning. He was nearly forty years old and still looking forward to someday. "It's a condition my relatives are eager to remedy, but I'm . . . still waiting."

She nodded her understanding. She had impatient relatives, and she was waiting too. The waiting was the hardest to bear.

His thoughts gravitated back to his father and getting to the hospital as quickly as possible. He glanced at his watch and made an impatient gesture as he recalled that time had stopped for him, minutes after he'd boarded the plane. Damn. And he'd just had the battery changed.

The plane touched down.

"I hate this part," she said, speaking loudly to be heard over the brakes and reverse thrusters. "There's so many more things for this plane to run into down here."

He smiled, amused, and almost as naturally as she'd come to his aid, he came to hers, squeezing her hand as it clutched the armrest between them. The effect, however, wasn't quite the same.

Skin touched skin, and subcutaneous nerve endings sizzled with excitement and pleasure. He tried patting her hand, but each touch sent a spasm of sensation up his arm. It was easier, more soothing, simply to submit and enjoy and wonder at the phenomenon.

She smiled at him tenuously. She wasn't sure which made her more nervous, the intimacy of his touch or land travel at air speed.

The plane began to taxi toward the terminal, and the moment was deliberately dismissed during the business of unfastening seat belts and wrestling carry-on luggage from under the seats in front of them.

The plane stopped, and as they waited on the edge of their seats to file out, she turned to him on impulse and said, "It was nice talking to you. My name is Holly Loftin."

"Oliver Carey," he said, smiling, liking her as much as he'd liked any complete stranger in a very long time. "Have a good Thanksgiving with your family."

The Carey name was familiar to her, but . . . well, it would have been too much of a coincidence. Surely there were many Careys not related to the Carey Foundation —tons of Careys. The Careys she was thinking of would never fly coach, no matter how desperate they were. They'd have private planes.

"Thanks," she said, dismissing the notion entirely. Then, because she felt as if she ought to say something positive and nothing about his father's ailment would have been, she added, "God bless you," thinking it would pretty much cover everything she wished for him.

He hadn't thought about God in ages, he realized. Not really. He followed her as she followed the fat woman into the aisle. Why hadn't she said, "God bless your father"? or "Good luck with your father"? Or "I hope your father doesn't die this time"?

In Oliver's book, "God bless you" was a phrase worn

tissue-thin in airports and on street corners, at social functions and at work, by overly enthusiastic born-again religious extremists. It had become as overused, impersonal, meaningless, and tiresome as "Have a nice day."

But when Holly Loftin said it, it became special and sincere, and it was sticking in his mind, playing over and over. And for no reason he knew, he took heart in it.

He stayed several steps behind her into the terminal, and though he was more concerned with getting to the main entrance than to the car rental or baggage claim area, he did notice that she didn't turn off in either of those directions either.

She was some distance ahead of him when it started. A rumbling from behind, as if a caravan of Mack trucks were barreling down the terminal toward him. The floor vibrated beneath his feet, harder and harder until it made his teeth rattle. He stepped to the wall to steady himself. It was shaking too. As many times as he'd experienced the tiny and not so tiny shifts of the San Andreas fault, it was always frightening and never predictable in its severity.

How long would it last? Should he run for an exit or stay where he was? Was he safe, or would he be buried under several tons of airport rubble? Before he could come to any decisions, the earthquake was over.

He was starting to look at the people around him when he glanced in Holly's direction. Whatever drew his attention to the ceiling above her would remain a mystery forever, but the crack and the widening gap, the specks of falling plaster, and Holly's bent head directly below, shot him into action.

"Holly!" he shouted, running toward her, bumping

into several other dazed people when they stepped into his path. "Get out of the way. Holly! Move!"

At the sound of her name, she looked around in a haze of confusion and residual fear. By the time she saw him and realized that he was coming at her, he was upon her. He grabbed her, and she instinctively resisted his attack. They tripped over each other's feet and fell, rolling and sprawling on the terminal floor as the ceiling came crashing in a few feet away.

Arms and legs entangled, they helped each other sit up. Through a cloud of plaster dust, Holly stared up at the enormous black cavity in the ceiling, then down at the pile of debris where she had been standing.

"That would've hurt," she said, speaking aloud the first coherent thought to enter her mind.

The understatement caught Oliver's fancy. He started to laugh, and once began, it was like a faucet for all his pent-up emotions. Grief. Sorrow. Fear. Relief. He laughed harder.

It was contagious. She grinned as she watched him, then chuckled, and before she knew it, she was giggling uncontrollably with tears in her eyes.

Tourists walked wide of them, staring, setting off new fits of chuckles. Every look at the hole in the ceiling was a fresh source of amusement. And trying to stand on fear-jellied knees was hilarious—not to mention brushing white plaster powder off each other's noses.

"Are you sure you're all right?" Oliver asked when he could stand *and* speak at the same time.

"Don't I look all right?" she asked, still chuckling as she tried to brush herself clean. "I feel great."

Airport personnel had arrived to inquire likewise and to begin cleaning up the mess.

"You're not hurt? Bruised? That was a hard fall we took."

"As falls go, it was the best I've ever taken," she said, straightening. Her expression sobered as she looked at him. "You saved my life."

"No." He knew what was coming.

"Yes you did. I owe you my life."

"No you don't," he said quickly.

"I do. But since you already have a life, help me think of some other way to repay you."

"There's no need. Really," he said, uncomfortable with her gratitude. "I'm just glad that I saw the ceiling cracking before it fell. I'm glad you're okay."

He handed her the tote bag she'd been carrying and looked around for his carryall. It lay where he'd dropped it when he'd started after her.

"I know," she said, following him back toward his bag. "It's not much, but two of my brothers own Spoleto's. Do you know it?"

"I've heard of it."

"It's the best Italian restaurant outside Rome, and I want you to come. Just tell them who you are, and they'll feed you the best meal you've ever had—on the house."

"That's not necessary. I was glad to do it and . . ." He was suddenly inspired. ". . . and besides, I owed you for your kindness on the plane. Let's say we're even."

"Are you kidding?" she asked, turning to chase after him in the opposite direction. "Empathizing with someone doesn't come close to saving someone's life. I empathize with people all the time. It's nothing."

"In my case, it was very much something. I needed . . ."

"Whoa!" she cried, reaching for him as the floor began to vibrate again. Automatically he took her in his arms, and they stood together, wide-eyed, as the earth trembled beneath them.

"Aftershock," he muttered seconds later.

"I know."

Through his suit jacket, she could feel his heart pounding close to hers. His arms felt like the safest place in the world.

Oliver had the oddest sensation that he'd held her close to him before. Not too tall or too short, not too fat or too thin, she was a perfect fit.

"Is someone picking you up?" he asked, holding her away from him. He felt an urgency to get her out of the airport and on her way to her family before anything else could happen.

"No. I'm taking a taxi."

"I should have a car waiting for me," he said. "I can take you to wherever you're staying."

"It's nice of you to offer, but I'll take a taxi."

He frowned. He hadn't expected a refusal. Who'd pay for a cab in L.A. when they could get a free ride? Surely she knew she'd be safe in a car with him.

"You need to be with your father," she said, setting his thoughts straight once again.

He nodded, feeling a clear and unforeseen sense of sadness at having to leave her.

"So, it's good-bye . . . again," he said, his hands falling to his sides.

She nodded and, after a few jerky movements, extended her hand to him, saying, "Thank you. For saving my life."

"You're welcome. It was well worth the effort."

The handshake was warm and strong—and enduring.

She accompanied him to the front of the airport, smiled, and said good-bye one last time, then continued down the walk to the cab stand.

But she didn't walk alone. She could feel his presence beside her. She sensed that he was still with her. Her skin prickled, as if he were touching her.

She looked back, and though the distance was great and the pedestrian traffic obscured a complete and steady view of him, he was standing in the crowd, watching her.

A pleased sort of warmth settled in her heart. People had a way of coming and going in her life. Some left vivid images on her consciousness. Others faded to vague, dreamlike memories. A few passed through unnoticed.

When she thought about such things as life and death and the impact she made on other people's lives, she always wanted to be a vivid image. In some small way, she wanted to leave a part of herself in everyone she touched, to achieve immortality in their memory.

She would be a vivid image to Oliver Carey, she knew. They wouldn't meet again, but he'd never forget her. With one tiny, effortless act of charity, she had carved a place for herself in his memory that would last forever. Recollections of his father were lifelong in the making, yet every time he thought of his father, he would remember Holly's kindness as well.

As for Holly, well, how could she possibly forget the

man who had saved her life? They had forged a definite bond that day, and she was well pleased.

She raised her arm high in the air, and after a brief moment he did the same, then disappeared into the crowd.

TWO

The scent of fresh-baked bread laced with garlic and oregano wasn't what most people would consider the traditional aroma of Thanksgiving, but it was for Holly.

It brought to mind a big table surrounded by the faces of people she loved. In her head she could hear them laughing and talking. In her heart she could relive the impressions of being safe and wanted.

"Nepotism never works," Tony Spoleto said, wrapping an arm about Holly's neck and squeezing playfully. "The help isn't worth day old pasta. It stands around daydreaming and lets the bread get cold."

Holly laughed and waited to be released before she slid her arm around his waist, saying, "It's also cheap and cheerful. Besides hot bread, what more could you ask for?"

"Speed?" he asked, grinning. "Did Mama leave already?" he asked, scanning the full-to-capacity restaurant —plus three extra tables—that he and his brother owned and operated 365 days a year.

"Bobby took her home a little while ago," she said, looking specifically at the tables in her section. "She said you had a good crowd this year and the cannelloni was overcooked."

"It wasn't." He was outraged. He'd grown up speaking mostly Italian at home. And though he spoke perfect English when he wanted to, he preferred to use the more impassioned broken English of his parents for atmosphere. "What does she know, huh? She gets older and older every year."

Holly smiled. Some things never changed. Marie Spoleto's boys had talked irreverently about their mama since the day Holly met them—always behind her back and always with great affection.

"Who would know better?" she asked. "It is her recipe, isn't it?"

"Yeah, yeah. Someone teaches you how to cook, and for the rest of your life she's telling you the cannelloni is overcooked," he said, his speech passionate, his eyes amused. "Go wait on a table or something. It's not good to see the help standing around with nothing to do."

He gave her shoulder a fond and indulgent squeeze, then disappeared into the kitchen—to check the cannelloni, no doubt.

She turned to prepare a tray of coffee and espresso for a table of six. She sensed his presence before she heard his voice.

Like the flash from a bolt of lightning, he appeared vivid and sharp in her thoughts. For no reason she knew of, her chest grew tight and achy with emotions she couldn't decipher. Then she heard it. A voice. It came softly but clearly from a distance. A familiar voice. A voice she was glad to hear. A voice that eased the discomfort around her heart.

She turned her head and she saw him halfway across the room.

So, Oliver Carey had decided to take her up on the free dinner she'd promised him for saving her life. She was pleased. She wanted everything to be perfect for him and his guests, an elderly lady and two very beautiful young women, she noted with no little interest.

She'd told Marie Spoleto and her brothers about Oliver Carey at supper the night she'd arrived. They would be happy to see and meet him also, for, as they frequently said, Holly was their favorite girl.

"Louis," she hissed, motioning frantically with her hand to a man in his mid-forties. Louis was headwaiter, wine steward, maitre d', and troubleshooter all rolled into a nice round little body, with sharp eyes and a bald top. He'd been at Spoleto's since the day before the grand opening. "Louis. Come here."

"What now?" he asked. His tone was gruff, but his presence was patient and obliging. "Have you lost a customer's credit card? Gotten your sleeve caught on a gentleman's toupee? Dumped antipasto down the front of a new bride?"

She grimaced, recalling each incident with humbling clarity. "I'm not much of a waitress, am I?"

"No. But you are . . . stimulating."

"I like your attitude, Louis." She grinned and stepped closer. "And if that's the way you're thinking, then I've been very dull tonight. So I'm going to pester you for a favor." He braced himself. "See that man over there? Red tie. Handsome. Dark hair. He's sitting with three ladies?" He nodded. "He's a friend of mine, and I'd like you to give his table lots of special attention."

"I give excellent service to all the customers."

"I know that. But he's special."

"How special?" he asked with a raised brow, as avidly interested in her life as her family was.

"His father is ill and he needs some cheering up," she said. Louis was a devout romantic. She didn't want him to read anything into her request that wasn't there.

"Why don't you take him?"

"I don't want him to feel uncomfortable, or as if he has to talk to me every time I go to the table. I'll serve coffee later and say hello then."

He studied her face with narrowed eyes, then patted her cheek. "I'll make him feel like a king," he said, then added, "You are a good girl, Holly."

A good girl, she thought, watching him approach Oliver's table. Always a girl. Never a woman in their eyes. She shook her head at the strangeness people called life. She had been eight years old when she'd moved into the Spoleto household. Frightened. Insecure. Unloved. They had taken her to their collective bosom in a greedy embrace. They had loved her hard and fast, made her feel special, raised her healthy and whole. But she'd had to move to San Francisco to feel like a woman. Independent. Freethinking. Capable of making her own life and living with her own mistakes.

They were family, and she loved coming home to wallow in the luxury of being treated as a cherished pet for a while. But just once she'd like to hear one of them say that they'd created a fine woman, instead of a good girl.

She kept a close eye on Oliver and his lady friends. She managed to stay at his back or with her back to him, leaning low to talk to the patrons as if she had laryngitis.

Louis was a pro. He complimented Oliver. He flirted with the ladies. He entertained them with amusing anecdotes and served their meal with great aplomb. She could see that Oliver was enjoying himself. His smile was like a beacon that lit every corner of the room. He was animated and cordial with all three ladies, though to Holly's eye the blonde at the table seemed a little overly cordial in return. Only occasionally would Holly catch a sad, somber look in Oliver's eyes. In those brief moments, she would know he was thinking of his father, and her heart would reach out to him.

"Hello, Oliver," she said, coming to stand at his table when they had finished their meal. She carried a coffee tray with both hands. Her hands were trembling a bit, and she wasn't taking any chances with a mishap. Not with Oliver. Please God, not with Oliver. "I'm glad to see you changed your mind."

"Holly," he said, surprised, getting to his feet to greet her. "I didn't. I mean, I didn't change my mind. I hadn't planned to come. This is sort of a . . . a coincidence. What are you doing here?"

"Serving coffee. Please. Sit down." She set a cup of espresso in front of the blonde and served the others coffee, Oliver last.

"Do you work here? I thought you were only visiting," he asked, hardly blinking while he watched her circle the table in a pseudo-tuxedo that made her seem a little taller than he remembered.

She looked down into his face and grinned. Her insides lurched abruptly. She reached out to straighten the small cornucopia centerpiece.

"It's sort of a busman's holiday. I'm going home tomorrow. How was your dinner?"

"You were right. It was the best Italian food I've eaten outside Rome."

"You've been to Rome?"

"A couple of times," he said, amused by her surprise, inordinately happy to see her.

If she were a snappy tune, he would have found himself humming it a hundred times since they'd parted at the airport. He'd thought about her over and over during the long hours in the hospital waiting room. Wondering who she was and what she was doing was a harmless haven of distraction in a sea of misery and heartache. But it was with the assumption that he'd never see her again.

It had seemed only natural that when Johanna suggested Spoleto's for dinner, he readily agreed. But it had been with the simple idea of connecting with something she was connected to; perhaps to see a member of her family—someone who might look like her; to learn a bit more about her. He hadn't dared to hope she'd be there.

Though why he would hope at all, he wasn't sure. He wasn't fall-on-his-face infatuated with her. She was just a woman he'd met on an airplane. A nice woman. A kind woman. An appealing woman. But certainly no one to get brain-bogged about.

Speaking of brain-bogged, he suddenly remembered his companions.

"Holly, this is my aunt, Elizabeth Carey George. Her daughter, my cousin, Johanna Reins. And a family friend, Babs Renbrook."

She recognized Ms. Renbrook from the society pages, now that she'd heard her name. Elizabeth Carey George suddenly had a face to go with a name she'd heard many times before. It was with a mixture of pleasure, resentment, and intrigue that Holly connected Oliver Carey to a world she touched every day, battled with constantly, and could never be a part of.

"Barbara," the socialite corrected him, her voice as sweet as church music—a divergence from the hard, possessive glint in her eyes.

"This is Holly, uh . . ." He knew every detail of her face, but couldn't remember her last name? Odd. But then, what was a name compared to bronze-colored eyes that seemed to look gently and fondly on the world from the center of time?

"Loftin. Holly Loftin," she said, unperturbed.

"We met on the plane coming down and screamed together during the earthquake." They exchanged secret smiles.

"I'm pleased to meet you," she said to the ladies.

Elizabeth George shook her perfect silver coiffure. "Why your father insists on living down here is beyond me," she said to Oliver, ignoring Holly. "Palm Springs is nothing but a showcase of wealth and decadence. We don't have nearly as much trouble with the earthquakes at home."

He gave his aunt a sharp look, then turned back to Holly.

"How is your father?" she asked before he could speak.

"He's holding on," he said, responding to her inquiry as he might to an old and dear friend's. "He's in pain, but

they keep him pretty well medicated. He sleeps a lot."
He smiled. "He sent us away this afternoon. I think we
make him nervous, hovering around as if we're waiting
for him to die."

"Oliver!" Elizabeth admonished.

Truth to tell, Holly couldn't blame Oliver's father for
being nervous under the eye of the watchful women. She
was too. With the exception of Oliver and his cousin,
Johanna, who sat with a quiet, polite smile on her face,
she was getting the distinct impression that she was not a
welcome addition to the party.

"We decided to go out for a nice family Thanksgiving
dinner," he said. "But none of us felt much like eating
turkey. Johanna's been here before and wanted to come
back—"

"She gets her craving for spicy foods from her father," Elizabeth injected derisively.

"It's my favorite restaurant," Johanna said softly,
smiling at Holly.

"I'll tell my brothers." She smiled back.

"Your family owns this establishment?" Barbara
asked, her expression cool. She glanced from side to side
beneath thick dark lashes at the chic surroundings, as if
the restaurant's popularity could only be some sort of
fluke, now that she'd met part of the management. "And
the whole family works here?"

"No," she said, feeling as if she were taking an oral
test. "I mean, yes, two of my brothers own it, but we
don't all work here."

"We . . . all?"

Holly recognized the intonation in her voice. Growing up in a large family, she was accustomed to the envy

of some, the awe of others, and the disgust of a few who would automatically assume that Marie Spoleto had a problem with birth control.

She drew her head up high and tried to be as civil as possible, for Oliver's sake.

"I have ten brothers, Ms. Renbrook. There are only three left here in town, and the rest are scattered across the country as far away as New York. Two are doctors, one's a lawyer, one teaches at MIT, two own this restaurant, another owns a hardware store, another designs cars for Chrysler, and the other two own the Spoleto Construction Company in Atlanta. So, you see, we don't all do menial labor. Just me."

"And that's only until tomorrow," Johanna said, stepping in cheerfully. "Where is home, Holly?"

"This is home, but I live in Oakland now."

"Really? We do too. Well, San Francisco, but what's the difference?" she said.

With the Bay between them, Oakland was to San Francisco as Queens and the Bronx were to Manhattan. A part of the whole but never thought to be the best part or even a part worthy of belonging to the whole. The differences were enormous, but it was nice that Johanna didn't think so.

"Which restaurant do you work in there?" she asked.

"I don't," Holly said, liking Johanna almost as much as she liked Oliver, who was sitting quietly at her elbow, watching her. Needing something to do with her hands, she blindly added cream to Oliver's coffee. "I come down two days before Thanksgiving every year to put up my mother's Christmas lights—on her house, you know? Then I work here on Thanksgiving because of the crowd, and to pay for the plane fare back, and to be with my family, of course."

"Couldn't one of your many brothers put up your mother's house lights?" Elizabeth asked, with an obvious disdain for gaudy decorations. However, her curiosity was mere and mild compared to her interest in Oliver's coffee—into which Holly added two white packets of sugar. "Aren't there ladders involved? I believe most people would hire someone to do it."

The Spoleto family finances were no one's business but their own, but the woman's attitude was irksome.

"They could do it, I suppose, or even hire someone. But I've always done it. And ladders don't bother me."

"Then do you come back for Christmas too?" Johanna asked, also watching Oliver's coffee. Holly stirred it, then slid it closer to him without looking.

"No. I do something else at Christmas, but I come back in the spring and again about midsummer."

"What service," Barbara exclaimed dryly, making a point of Oliver's coffee cup.

Holly frowned and looked, then gasped in horror when she realized what she'd done.

"Oliver, I'm so sorry," she said, quickly taking the cup away, thinking Louis would be glad to know that the evening wouldn't be tediously dull after all. "I'll get you a fresh cup and—"

"No. No," he said, taking her free hand. "That's exactly the way I drink it." He chuckled. "I was just trying to figure out how you knew I took cream and two packets of sugar and not artificial sweetener. I must have taken it that way on the plane. No, I . . ." He frowned.

"You had a drink on the plane," she said.

"Yes, I did," he said, puzzled. "Jack Daniels."

He continued to look at her, a baffled smile on his lips as he recalled the drink she'd given him and his quiet surprise that she'd chosen his preferred brand. And now her strange knowledge of his coffee-drinking habits . . .

"Weird, huh?" she asked, moving her gaze from the cup to his face. She wasn't reading his mind, was she? He didn't believe in such stuff, but still, she had an uncanny way of responding to things he was thinking about. "Or are you just saying you drink it like this to be nice?" she asked.

"Oliver? Nice?" Barbara chuckled, sounding as if she thought Oliver couldn't be nice. The notion rang a familiar bell with Holly. Her first impression of him was that he might be a rather severe sort of person, but as he'd been nothing but kind and gentle with her, she took instant umbrage to the inference.

Oliver didn't notice it.

"Truly," he said, squeezing her wrist gently, reassuringly. "This cup is fine. Perfect."

"Okay." She nodded feebly. "Then if there's nothing else I can get you, I'll leave you to finish. It was nice to meet you," she said to the ladies in general, with a special smile for Johanna. "It's been nice seeing you again, Oliver. I'm glad you came."

"I am too," he said, and then he watched her walk away.

"Not much room to kick yourself in here," Holly muttered to herself, glancing at the walls of the employee's rest room/lounge that wasn't much bigger than a closet. She bent to splash cold water on her face.

The thing with Oliver's coffee had been bad enough, but it hurt in a way that was totally unreasonable that his family hadn't liked her. Except Johanna. Who seemed to be a very kind person—which meant she wouldn't show her dislike of a stranger if she had any, anyhow.

She shouldn't have gone to the table. She should have left Oliver in peace to enjoy his meal with his family and his friend and not have been so stupid and self-indulgent as to intrude on his privacy.

Who was she to him after all? A person he'd met on an airplane. She should have been grateful that he'd remembered her name. Well, part of her name, anyway.

"Holly?"

She frowned. For a moment she thought she'd conjured up his voice at the door.

"Holly? Are you in there?"

"Oliver?"

"Yes. Will you come out? Or . . . or can I come in there?"

She opened the door to face him. She wasn't going out and she wasn't letting him in, but she couldn't have him speaking through the door at her.

"Hi," he said gently. Because he wasn't sure of what he was seeing, he tipped her chin upward with two fingers. "Have you been crying?"

"No. I burnt my finger in the kitchen," she said, hiding her perfectly fine index finger in the palm of her other hand. "It smarts."

"Let me take a look. How bad is it? I'll get some ice—"

"No. It's fine. I'm clumsy. I burn myself all the time. What are you doing back here?"

"Oh," he said, recalling the reason himself. "Louis told me where to find you. He . . . he won't give me our bill. He says it's on the house, which is very nice of you, but I really can't let you do that."

"Why not? I invited you here for a free dinner. I know it isn't much, but . . . you saved my life."

"That was my privilege," he said, his eyes roving over every inch of her face, enjoying every simple detail for the hundredth time. "I don't need to be paid for it."

"But I feel indebted. So do my brothers. And my mother. Besides, who's going to miss four plates of Italian food in a place like this? Please, it's a small price to pay for my life."

"All right," he said, giving in and not liking it. "But I insist on paying the bar tab. That wasn't part of the deal."

Before she could stop him, he was reaching inside his suit jacket for his wallet. He tried the other side and his pants pockets before he looked at her, embarrassed to the bone.

"I don't have my wallet," he said.

"You see," she said brightly, feeling for him. "It's fate. Destiny knew you weren't going to need it tonight, so she let you leave it at home."

"I can't even pay you with a credit card," he said, shamefaced.

She laughed.

"Oliver Carey, you're a very stubborn man," she said, stepping out of the rest room. She couldn't stop the hand that reached out to touch him. "If you don't let me do this for you, all of it, the whole bill, I'm going to tell my brothers that you're here." She made it sound worse than facing a firing squad. "I was going to spare you that. They're full-blooded Italians and very emotional, and they love me very much. Your worst nightmare won't compare to the stink they'll make over you for saving their favorite girl's life."

He grinned and let her turn him back through the kitchen toward the restaurant.

"You're your brothers' favorite girl?" he asked, intrigued by the wording.

"The family's token girl," she said, lighthearted, tucking her arm into the bend of his as they walked. "Marie Spoleto is my foster mother, and four of my brothers are actually other children she adopted and raised alongside her own six boys. Let's see, does that make eleven of us? Yes. I was the last one she took in, and, of course, the joke at home goes two ways—either I was the girl she'd been wanting all along, or once she got me, she couldn't tolerate any more children."

He chuckled with her. "Were you a little handful?" he asked, thinking she must have been. Wishing he knew firsthand.

"No. I was shy and quiet most of the time."

"Who is this you're talking about?" Tony asked, coming into the kitchen from behind them. "Not yourself, I hope. She lies all the time," he told Oliver with a twinkle in his eye. "She was the worst. A terror. My mama turned gray overnight."

"She was gray when I got here, from raising you."

He nodded the sad truth to Oliver, saying, "My mama is a crazy old woman. She raises her children, gets sad when they leave her, and goes out to find five more to raise. Me?—I want to kill my two children twice a day. Who is this?" he asked, turning abruptly back to Holly.

With an evil smirk on her lips she looked questioningly to Oliver, who gave her a sharp quailing stare.

"This is a friend of mine from San Francisco, Tony. Oliver Carey, my brother Antonio Spoleto. Bobby is around here too someplace, but Tony doesn't get quite so personal with his interrogations."

"Interrogations?" Tony looked shocked. "What she means is that I'm never anything but pleasant and charming with my inquiries," he said calmly. "So, what kind of a friend from San Francisco are you, Oliver Carey?"

"You have the right to remain silent," Holly said. "You have the right to an attorney. . . ."

"Okay, okay," Tony said, laughing. "No questions. She confuses our loving concern with being nosy." He poinked her on the nose. "Growing up in our family hasn't always been easy for this girl."

"It was always easy," she said. "But annoying sometimes."

"Holly's very proud of her family," Oliver said. "You can tell when she talks about you."

"Awk"—he covered his ears as if they had suddenly caught fire—"I can hear her now," he said, then added, "You take your friend's bill, okay? He eats on the house. And now I'm going to find my big brother Roberto, to tell him we have a friend of our girl in the restaurant."

"You better hurry, Oliver. Bobby'll want to know everything from your social security number to your intentions toward me."

"It must be nice to be loved by so many."

"It is." She pushed him through the kitchen door into the restaurant. "One thing I know about is love."

"I like your brother."

"Me too," she said, pushing him toward his table.

"Are they all like him?"

"Yes. Some are worse."

He turned and wouldn't let her push him any farther.

"Thank you for dinner," he said formally, then more personally he went on, "Thank you for the plane ride. Thank you . . ." *just for being here tonight,* he was about to say. "Well, just thanks. I won't forget you."

"I know you won't." Her smile was sagacious.

"Look," he said with a hesitation he was unaccustomed to and couldn't appreciate. "Here's my card if you ever . . . if you ever need anything or . . . if you feel like getting together for a drink or something sometime. I'd . . . I'd like to see you again."

"Thanks." She took the card. It seemed like a very upper-class thing to do, handing out cards. Aside from his wallet, Oliver Carey appeared to have everything. Wealth. Privilege. Sophistication. Yet there was a great need in him that pulled at her. And she sensed that before long his need would become even greater. "When you're . . . well, I'm in the book, if you want to talk to me."

THREE

Holly Loftin was never home. She didn't sleep. And she never used her telephone. Oliver knew these things for certain, because he'd called her apartment fifty times over the past two weeks. The line was never busy and she never picked up, even when he called after midnight.

He wasn't used to people being unavailable to him, and it was damned irritating—in an illogical, irrational sort of way.

She did have an answering machine. Loath to admit it, he'd called several times simply to hear her voice, but he hadn't left a message. What could he say?

"Holly, my father died and you were the first person I thought of . . . actually, the only person I thought of?"

"Holly, I need to talk?"

"Holly, we buried my father today, and I know this is going to sound really perverted because we hardly know each other, but I was wondering if you might be willing to hold me for an hour or two?"

"Holly, my father is gone and I think about you constantly"?

"Holly, I'm lonely. Where are you?"

He'd tried every missive out loud, but couldn't bring himself to leave them on the machine.

With every passing day and with every beep from her machine, his need to see her escalated beyond desire and longing, beyond craving, to a point that found him leaving work on Friday, taking the top deck of the Bay Bridge straight into the heart of Oakland, then driving up and down quiet, Christmas-frilled neighborhood streets with every intention of camping on her doorstep until she finally came home.

"Who is it?" she called through the door when he knocked.

He was so shocked to hear her voice, it took him a second or two to answer. The door was draped with a glittering gold garland and tiny bright lights. An extension cord ran thirty feet down the hall to light them up. It had to be her.

"Oliver Carey," he said.

"Oh, Oliver!" she said, and he was pleased to hear the excitement in her voice. "Don't move. I'm not dressed. Don't go away. I'll only be a second." A pause. "I'm so glad you've come."

Still a bit perturbed, he was about to tell her that he'd have come sooner if she'd answer her phone once in a while, but decided to wait until she opened the door. Which would happen at any second if the running footsteps from inside were any indication.

The muffled cries of a baby drew his attention down the corridor, beyond the extension cord. The walls were drab and dirty. Someone was listening to the evening news on television, and the air reeked of long-gone cooking.

It wasn't the sort of place he frequented. And he hadn't pictured Holly living in quite so impoverished a state. It wasn't the first time that he realized how little he knew about her. He recalled that she'd said she didn't wait tables for a living, so what did she do? Did her brothers know she lived liked this? If Spoleto's Restaurant was any indication, they had plenty of money. Why didn't they help her out a little financially? Did it ever frighten her to live in such a place, alone and unprotected?

Of course, when Holly whipped open the door, every thought in his head was blown away, save one.

She was naked. Well, she'd said as much when he knocked, but . . . and . . . well, she hadn't covered much up in the meantime.

She stood barefoot before him, wearing nothing but a slip, panties, and a huge smile.

The slip was black silk, and though it had straps, it seemed to be clinging precariously low along the firm rounded swell of her breasts, as if any draft could send it floating to the floor. Lower there was a faint outline of skimpy underpants and that was all . . . except for the words.

In white, the words *mother*, *father*, *toilet*, *thumb*, *dreams*, and a couple more that curved around to the back, were affixed somehow to the slip.

"Oliver, I'm so happy to see you. How are you?" she said immediately. "I saw the notice about your father in the paper, and I've been so worried about you. I tried to call a couple of times but . . . well, it doesn't matter now."

She reached out and led him into her apartment as if she were dressed to the nines and showing him in to tea. His stunned expression must have caused her to add, "It doesn't matter how prepared you think you are for something like this, it's always a shock when it actually happens, isn't it?"

"Yes. It is," he said, his mouth dry as a cotton ball. He could see the impression of her nipples in the silk—which was nothing compared to the impression they were making in his mind. "I . . . seem to have come at a bad time," he said, motioning to her attire—or lack thereof.

"Bad time?" She looked confused and then down at her costume and laughed. "No. It's not a bad time. Please. Come in and sit down. I was getting ready to go to a party, but I still have a while and . . . What?"

"You're going to a party like that?"

She smiled as she recognized the expression on his face. It was the same rather annoying mask of dubious disapproval her brothers wore when they thought her hems were too high, her neckline too low, her jeans too tight. Except that on Oliver the guise was sort of endearing, even flattering because he looked a little nervous as well.

"Like what?"

"Well . . . dressed like that?"

"Of course not. I'll put on shoes."

"Shoes?" He looked at her feet. They weren't knobby or pointed or calloused or bony. They were soft and rounded and sexy as hell to Oliver, who until that moment hadn't considered a foot fetish a creditable fixation.

"I still need to do my hair too."

Her hair looked fine. Shiny and beautiful.

"I thought I'd wear it up, so it wouldn't distract attention from my costume," she said, lifting her arms, her breasts following the motion as she piled her dark hair on the top of her head. "What do you think?"

Oliver wasn't thinking. His fingers were tingling and his insides felt like so many knots in a shoestring, and the familiar pressure between his legs was growing faster and stronger than he'd ever known it to before. But he wasn't *thinking* anything.

"That's a costume?" he asked, brows lifted, his hands trembling enough to warrant holding them behind him.

He wasn't stupid or being naive. He knew she was teasing him. She was flaunting herself sexually in a counteraction to his reaction to her. She was getting the better of him, too, and she knew it, and was enjoying herself immensely.

"Don't you like it?"

What wasn't to like?

"Sure, I like it, but . . . what's it for?"

"I told you. I'm going to a party," she said, laughing. "A costume party. One of those annual Christmas things for charity. You know, where people dress up and give money?"

"Yes. I'm familiar with the concept." To the tune of thousands of dollars every year, he thought, wondering why he hadn't ever gotten an invitation to an underwear event for any of the charities he supported. He was sure they'd be vastly more interesting than the black-tie affairs he usually attended.

"Why don't you come with me?" she said suddenly.

"It's an amateur art auction and costume party for St. Augustine's Convalescent Center. You like art. You should come."

He did like art, but it wouldn't occur to him until sometime later to wonder how she knew. At present he was far too busy trying to visualize himself at an art auction in his underwear.

"I don't think so," he said, with more regret than he imagined for such a ridiculous notion. He was no puritan, but there were some things he simply couldn't bring himself to do. "Thanks, but I'm not . . ."

"In a party mood?" she asked sympathetically, the light in her eyes no longer merry and playful but brimming with understanding and compassion. She smiled at him, and for a long instant he was tempted to throw caution to the wind, along with his suit, and spend the night with her at the party. Bring her home afterward. Invite himself in for a nightcap. He pictured himself with a drink in his hand, moving slowly toward her in the dimly lit room. . . .

"Would you like something to drink?" she asked, startling him.

It was becoming too weird, the way she'd make a remark or ask a question about something that was touching his mind; the way she knew his tastes without previous exposure to them. It was beginning to give him the creeps.

"No. Thanks. I don't want to keep you. I just stopped by to see you. To see how you were."

"Sit down, Oliver," she said softly. "I know why you came, and I'm very glad you did." She pressed him back into a chair, saying, "I'll get us something hot to drink, and then we'll talk. How does sweet lemon tea sound?"

He didn't know what it was, but it sounded wonderful . . . although watching her walk away was slightly more wonderful.

Holly had the water in the kettle before she decided to act on the impulse to tell Oliver something few people knew about her. She stepped back into the archway and watched as he idly examined the books on her coffee table, smoothed the crease in his pants, and tapped his fingers on the armrest. He sighed. Smiled at her foot-high Christmas tree. Closed his eyes. Then leaned his head back against the chair.

It wasn't hard for her to imagine what he was thinking about. And it wasn't her. His sadness was like a tangible thing in the room, another entity that stayed close to his side, a constant companion. It would wander off when Oliver's mind was diverted, but once he lost interest, it came back to pester and bedevil him.

"It's not a terrible thing, you know," she said.

"What?" he asked, nearly jumping out of his skin. And if she said anything about his father, he was going to scream and start running.

"Dying. It's not a terrible thing."

She spoke with such candor and sureness that he opted to scream and run later.

"Are you speaking from experience?" he asked warily, a skeptic to most things that couldn't be seen, heard, or felt in some way.

"Yes."

He studied her for a moment, then stood and walked

toward her, saying, "You've died and come back, then. You've had one of those out-of-body experiences?"

"No. I mean, yes, I did die. I was clinically dead for almost eight minutes. But I don't remember tunnels and lights, if that's what you mean."

"What happened?"

"How did I die? Or what happened that makes me so sure that dying isn't a terrible thing?"

"Both."

When she turned and went back into the tidy kitchen, he followed her, stepping around a ten-speed bicycle, which was a little odd to see in a living room—but no more odd than anything else where she was concerned.

Holly didn't like talking about the incident. Something about it always made her feel completely vulnerable and out of control. And it was a private thing, a matter of the heart that she didn't want exposed to question or ridicule. She would tell Oliver this truth as she knew it, to ease his pain. Whether he chose to believe her or not was up to him.

"Three years ago I had an allergic reaction to penicillin. The doctor said it was something like a tolerance overload. I'd taken it all my life for bad colds and infections, and all along I'd been gradually building up these allergens to it. He also said it wasn't an uncommon thing to happen, but usually the symptoms were as gradual as the overload and they generally detected it sooner. It just didn't happen that way in my case."

"What did happen?"

She shrugged. The before part was a matter of record and easy to talk about.

"I let myself get run down and caught a cold, and

then I didn't take care of it," she said easily. "Before long I was a case of walking pneumonia. The doctor wanted to put me in the hospital, but I didn't have time for that, so he injected me with a starter dose in the office and sent me home with a fistful of prescriptions for cough syrup and nose stuff and, of course, more penicillin."

She stirred a homemade tea concoction and the boiling water into a teapot and went on, "When I first had trouble breathing, I didn't think too much of it. I did have pneumonia, after all, and it wasn't much worse than before, except that I thought I was getting better. I kept thinking I was having a relapse, that it would pass in a day or two. I even went to work."

She took two thick mugs from the cupboard and poured equal amounts of tea into each, handing one to Oliver. It smelled like citrus and spices, fresh and cloying at once.

"I took another pill before I went on my dinner break, and an hour later I passed out cold. Then my heart stopped. The paramedics did CPR and defibrillated me a couple of times in the ambulance on the way to the hospital. I still have little scars from where the paddles burned me, but . . . I was long gone by the time we got there."

"And then, suddenly, you were back?"

She chuckled because it did sound funny—truth was strange that way.

"That's pretty much how it happened. Somewhere in the move from the ambulance to the emergency room, I developed a pulse. They took turns guessing at the cause. Hard bumping and jarring of the stretcher. A buildup and sudden release of adrenaline. A muscle contraction. A full moon. A miracle."

"Maybe they were mistaken. What if your pulse was so weak, they couldn't feel it? Maybe you weren't dead after all?"

"Maybe," she conceded, but in her heart she knew different.

"What did it feel like?" he asked, taken in by her story.

This was the hard part. She slid into a straight-backed chair at the table, cupping the mug with her hands as she sought the proper words. Oliver did the same.

"Physically, I was still sicker than a dog. On top of the pneumonia, I was throwing up and shaking all over. I was miserable, but"—she frowned—"inside, deep down, like in my soul or in the deepest part of my mind, I knew that those eight minutes were something special and wonderful . . . that I'd spent them with something glorious and good. I woke up with an unshakable belief in God— or at least a higher power of some sort. *And* I was certain of the existence of a life after death. Something I was never sure of before."

She went silent for a moment, and when Oliver seemed willing to hear more without comment, she went on.

"Even though I don't remember any details, like tunnels and lights or floating over my body, I do remember that as wretched as I felt when I woke up, I was as happy and at peace on the other side."

Oliver remained quiet and contemplative for several minutes, lost in thoughts she could not touch or imagine.

She propped her head on her fist and sat with him, open and ready to share the burdens of his heart.

"Do you suppose it's like that for everyone?" he asked finally.

"Yes. Everyone. Good people. Bad people. We all go to the same place."

"No hell? No eternal suffering?"

She shook her head, sorry to disappoint him. "Nothing but goodness."

"Then what's the point?"

"Beats me," she said truthfully.

"But you've had time to think about it; what do you think?"

"Based on what I know for sure, in my heart"—she placed an open hand over it—"and the explanations available, I'm leaning heavily toward reincarnation. There was nothing bad or evil where I went. Nothing. I didn't sense that there was more than one direction to go. Whatever it is, is. There is nothing else. And it's good. So, I think if you're a hurtful person in this life, you still go to where everyone else goes when you die. But when you come back, you suffer. Likewise, the less hurtful you are this time, the less you'll be hurt next time." He shouldn't have gotten her started. She leaned back in the chair and began her dissertation. "If you think about it, it works for entire nations if you want it to. Like if you're a conquering nation first, raping, pillaging, taking slaves . . . then you come back as part of an oppressed nation the next time. Or if you were a nation at war for several generations, then you come back fat and happy and live on farms in Kansas the next time, you see?"

He did, but he wasn't ready to make any quick decisions on her word alone. And that was fine. She could see that he'd taken her information and stockpiled it with whatever else he knew and believed and was willing to work with it. She was glad she'd told him.

He liked the sound of her voice, he decided. Not high and irritating or low and sultry, but moderate and soothing, with swift, subtle variations of emotions that were both pleasing and delightful.

Perhaps he wasn't as ready to discuss the mysteries of life as he'd thought he was? Just sitting there with her was enough to dispel the quandary in his mind and the ache in his heart. She'd made him feel good on the plane, and then at the restaurant. Maybe that's all he'd come for? To be with her and to feel good.

"This is good too," he said, lifting his cup of tea and draining it, changing the subject conspicuously. "What's in it?"

"Lemon, orange, cloves, cinnamon. . . . Are you sure you won't come to the party with me?" she asked, her smile enticing. She stood to rinse and set her cup in the sink. "I have a piece of art on display that you could bid on and pay an incredible amount of money for. There'll be food and lots of nice people." She turned to him with a brilliant piece of bribery. "I'll pay for your ticket."

He smiled and was severely tempted.

"I couldn't."

"Why not?"

"Well, look at you. I couldn't go out in public dressed like that."

"Of course you couldn't. This is my costume. We'd have to think up something else for you."

"What exactly is your costume?" he asked at last. She kept calling it a costume, but it still looked like lingerie to him.

"Guess," she said, her arms out as she turned slowly around before him. "I'll give you a hint. The theme this year is catchwords and phrases. I think I'm a phrase."

"A phrase."

"Go ahead, guess. What am I?"

What was she? Good question. His gaze shifted downward from the soft, gentle contours of her Mother Earth face, lingered briefly on her Venus de Milo breasts and her slim Cleopatra hips, slid down long, slender Amazonian legs to bare Pocahontas feet. Those were all famous women . . . wrong theme. He was beginning to enjoy the game as he started over from the top.

"Here's another clue," she said, pretending censure, her heart fluttering like the wings of a hummingbird. "Look at my costume, not my body."

"But I like looking at your body."

"So I've noticed," she said.

He grinned at her.

"Okay. Last clue," she said with a cheeky smile of her own, her eyes sparkling. "The key here is the words on the dress."

"That's a dress?"

"The words, Oliver. Concentrate on the words."

Father. Mother. Toilet. Thumb. Dreams. He wanted to concentrate on the words, but they dipped and curved over such nice hills and valleys. . . .

"It's a Freudian slip, Oliver," she said, trying to sound impatient as her nerves skittered and danced with excitement and her pulses tapped lively with anticipation. "I'm a Freudian slip. Get it?"

His grin stretched across his face. Merriment bubbled in his chest. And for the first time since the last time they'd laughed together there in the aftermath of an earthquake, he let loose a bellyful of guffaws that bounced off the walls and shook the windowpanes.

"Oh, Holly," he said, weak with laughter. "You are priceless. I never would have guessed it."

"Really?" She looked concerned. "I don't want to be a phrase no one will get."

"No. It's perfect. Great. Very clever. Lots of people will get it, and those that don't . . . well . . ." He made a vague gesture with his hands and went silent and sheepish.

"Those that don't, what?" she asked, suspicious.

"Well, those that don't get it aren't really looking at the costume. They're seeing other things."

"The way you were?"

Hmmm. He didn't like that thought one little bit. People looking at anything other than her costume. Come on. Be reasonable. Hell, she wasn't any of his business. What did he care if other men looked at her? Looked at . . . other things?

On the other hand, and if he cared to be truthful, there was a part of him that wanted her to be his business. All right. There was something about her that already was his business, though he wasn't sure what. And there was a lot more of her to see than a costume. Okay. So he cared.

"Come with me, Oliver," she coaxed.

"As what? What do Freudian slips take to parties?"

She beamed her happiness at his acceptance, then started looking around the room for his costume. She had it almost instantly.

"Here," she said, thrusting a box of breakfast cereal and a table knife at him. "It's you. Dark. Brooding. Mysterious."

"Come on, Holly. There's nothing dark, brooding, or mysterious about this." He looked down at the box in utter disgust. "I'm a flake."

"No you're not."

"I am. Look at me." He held out his arms with the cereal box in one hand and the knife in the other. "Everyone's going to know that I'm the flake with the Freudian slip."

"Not if you show them your knife. Then," she said, her eyes growing wide with fear, "everyone will know you're a serial killer."

FOUR

Oliver loved being a serial killer. It was the easiest disguise he'd ever worn. No plumes or fake mustaches. No tights or hot masks. He'd found his alter ego.

He would become darker, more brooding, and a whole lot less mysterious if someone had the nerve to suggest he was a flake, of course. But for the most part he played his role as the quiet, pleasant, next-door neighbor who was the last person anyone would have suspected of plotting the horrible demise of the next male he chanced to catch gazing a little too long at the Freudian slip.

Holly, as he might have guessed, was the center of attention. But it wasn't because of her costume.

He was quick to learn that Holly had instigated the annual amateur art auction and theme costume benefit five years earlier, when she'd first come to St. Augustine's. She'd coordinated it every year since, gradually increasing the accommodations to fit the ever-growing and remarkably distinguished guest list until it had become an event of some notoriety in the Oakland community.

"I had no idea Holly was importing her patrons from across the Bay already," commented a man at Oliver's back. "She works fast."

Oliver turned. Immediately he extended his hand in friendship to the long, lanky man wearing both a belt and suspenders to hold his pants up.

"Phil! How are you? I haven't seen you since . . . when? Last year?"

"At your aunt's do for some charity or another," he said, nodding. "In the spring. Great flower arrangements, as I recall."

It was an old joke, one they'd cultivated early in their relationship after having met in the shrubbery at a garden party. Since then they had shared other favorite hiding places at parties they hadn't particularly wanted to attend, such as the wall side of large potted plants, on the wrong side of vine-covered lattices, under the fall of a weeping willow, or behind any piece of furniture on which was set a prominent floral display.

"That's right. You took the one with the daffodils and hyacinths, and I got stuck with the big droopy pot of lilacs and had a crick in my neck for weeks," he said, laughing. "What are you doing here?"

"Having fun." He stepped back to observe Oliver's disguise. "What's this? Oh, I see. Cutting Corn-ers. Very clever."

Phil, despite the fact that he was a savvy owner of a chemical company that specialized in insecticides and was enormously wealthy, was also one of the gentlest, nicest, most down-to-earth people Oliver had ever met. However, his wit was a bit dull at times.

"Phil, I'm a serial killer."

Phil frowned and took another look, then he chuckled.

"Yes, indeed, I see it now. Very good. Now it's your turn," he said, holding up his belt with one hand and slipping the thumb of the other behind a suspender. "Guess what I am."

Oliver had discovered that keeping his guesses as simple as possible usually produced the correct answers. At present the only thing that came to mind was a very old joke he'd once heard.

"Are you a pessimist?"

"I knew I wouldn't fool anyone this way," he said, slipping easily into his shibboleth. "I swear, if I used saccharin, I'd get artificial diabetes; if I bought an unbreakable, waterproof, shockproof watch, I'd lose it; if I had my tailor make me two-pants suits, I'd burn holes in the jackets. . . ."

Oliver was in stitches. The jokes weren't as funny as Phil's uncharacteristic ease at being out-and-out silly. He'd never seen the man so relaxed and uninhibited.

Come to think of it, the whole gathering was one of friendly acquaintance between strangers. That the decorations were in a winter motif rather than Christmas, a sentimental season long noted for the spirit of *giving*, seemed to alleviate any pressure there might have been for the true purpose of the event. There was nothing stuffy or formal or proper or uncomfortable about it. Everyone was there to have fun, and that's exactly what they were doing—including Oliver.

". . . if I invested in General Motors, wagon trains would make a comeback; if I fell on my back, I'd break my nose. These are great, huh? I've got a hundred of them. I've been gathering them for weeks."

"Well, save a few for later," he said, giving Phil an affable pat on the back. "I want to know your connection to St. Augustine's. I might want to sign up."

"You already did."

"I did?"

"Well, your aunt and the pack she runs with did, and since she pretty much runs the fund-raising end for the Carey Foundation, I assume you did too."

Oliver was perplexed.

"Strange. I never heard of the place until tonight."

"Not strange, just not a popular cause. You don't see many news headlines about shut-ins picketing for better care. And the six o'clock news would rather show pictures of murdered bodies and beached whales getting put back to sea, than show what it's like when a dilapidated nursing home runs out of hot water or has a broken furnace."

"I didn't know this was a special interest of yours."

"I didn't know either, until I met Holly. Have you met Holly Loftin?"

"Yes."

Phil started to laugh. "Three years ago she crashed one of your aunt's operations and started recruiting contributors. She backed me into one of my hiding places and had me in tears by the time she was finished. Look there. She got Bill Gastrel that same night, and over there, see the hypochondriac with the thermometer behind his ear? You know Chevy Zamora, don't you?"

"Sure," he said, seeing several other familiar faces. "And who are the rest of these people? Locals?"

"Mostly. A few employees. A couple of residents. Trustees. Neighborhood folks. They do what they can, but we're the big bucks here."

"And Holly recruited you."

"Like a master sergeant. I was afraid *not* to come that first year. I was afraid she'd hunt me down again, but since then . . ." He paused and sobered. "I don't think there's anything I wouldn't do for that girl."

"Really?" he asked reflectively, wondering if she weren't some sort of witch who cast her magic spells on everyone she met. Wondering, too, if she knew his net worth. And since she seemed to make a point of knowing that sort of thing about certain people, why she hadn't hit him up for a donation.

"Oh, she's as plain as day about wanting my money, but she has a way of making me feel good about giving it. Not like it's a tax write-off, or my duty to do it. More like . . . well, hell, I don't know, just good about it. *And* she throws a hell of a party to boot."

"My ears are burning," she said from behind them. They parted to face her. "I hope you're not telling Oliver what a bloodsucking gold digger I am."

"I wouldn't think of it," Phil said, taking her hands and bending to plant an affectionate kiss on her cheek. Oliver wanted to do the same thing, but a little more to the left.

"Good. I wanted to thank you, too, for painting another picture for us this year. I like it even better than last year's. Did you know that Phil paints?" Oliver looked at the man as if he'd never met him before. "Wonderful pictures of children. Last year he did one of two little boys eating ice cream on a park bench that was so precious, I bid every dime of my savings for it. But Mrs. Vochec outbid me."

Oliver glanced back at Phil and almost dropped his teeth to see him blushing and simpering like a schoolboy. She was a witch.

"Tonight I slipped a magic sleeping potion into her punch that should take effect just about the time the auction starts," she said wickedly. "I'm not taking any chances this year."

Damn, she'd done it again. He was thinking witch, and she started talking potions. The tiny hairs on the back of his neck stood straight up.

Phil looked ready to bow his head and start shuffling his feet in the light of her admiration, so Oliver came to his rescue.

"Maybe I could talk you into taking me over and showing me some of this artwork?" he said. "Didn't you tell me you had a piece up too?"

"Yes, but mine is truly amateur compared to some, and nothing compared to Phil's."

"I'd like to see it, then. Both of them. I . . ." It was then that he recalled her earlier comment on his love of art. Had she been casing him, setting him up as a possible recruit? Was their meeting on the plane fixed or fate? Was that how she knew his tastes, seemed to read his thoughts, because she'd had him staked out all along? "I'm immune to magic potions and might have to outbid you tonight myself."

"Well, for the sake of St. Augustine's you're certainly welcome to try," she said, her smile wavering for a brief moment when she thought she saw a streak of anger in his eyes. "But I warn you, I'm very determined this year. I have more in my account than I had last year."

"Note taken," he said, fairly warned.

They made their excuses to Phil and began a slow migration to the art exhibit in an adjoining room. They could hardly take two steps without someone stopping Holly to congratulate her on the success of the party; to renew her acquaintance; to hug her warmly; to ask a question. It was extremely annoying.

Despite the circumstances, he couldn't shake the possessive notion that he was her escort for the evening. And he wasn't used to his date getting more regard than he got. She made a point of including him, but he could tell he didn't have her complete and undivided attention. And he wanted it. He had questions and he wanted answers.

It was irritating as hell not to be her focal point. Her friends were staring at him. Not as if he had money hanging out of his ears, he knew that stare. This was different. They were inspecting him. They were testing him with their remarks and rejoinders. They were auditing *his* worthiness to be with her.

Overall, he'd have to say that since his little discussion with Phil, he was feeling more and more like a serial killer—maladjusted, neurotic, and very dangerous.

Holly, who'd never been tuned in to anyone the way she was to Oliver, could feel the muscles in her shoulders contracting as he grew more and more stiff-necked beside her. The tension between them was like a live wire, snapping and throwing off sparks whenever they made contact. Something was different. And in her experience the fastest way to get a man's hackles up, to make him suddenly stiff and inflexible, was to wound his pride—which, unfortunately, was all too often connected in some way with his finances.

He followed her lead, bided his time, and took a distracted interest in each new piece of art as they circled the room. "Amateur" carried a wide definition—from comical to good to exemplary works that could hang in any number of professional galleries. Phil's, for instance, of two small children on their hands and knees exploring the life of a caterpillar, was remarkable. Stunning, really, if you knew the man who'd painted it.

Holly, who'd seen the display earlier, was far more interested in Oliver. Before her eyes he had become the man she'd glimpsed. Cool. Aloof. Unapproachable. Someone not nice, as if Barbara Renbrook's comment wasn't too far off the mark. Someone she couldn't like very much, and certainly wasn't comfortable being around.

When they'd gone far enough, she slipped her hand into his and pulled him through a metal doorway and into a hallway used by the hotel staff.

"Okay," she said, turning on him at once. "I know who you are, but I didn't until I met your aunt in L.A. The plane threw me off; I figured you'd own your own," she said in one breath. "Well, never mind that. . . . By the time I did realize who you were, I didn't think it really mattered. It certainly didn't to me. But to make this perfectly clear, you're welcome to make any donation you care to here tonight, but you don't *have* to leave a penny and that wasn't the reason I invited you. I'm not after your money. I don't care about your money. And if you still think differently, you can leave now."

She had the door open and was halfway through before he could stop her.

"You're very direct," he said, as surprised as he was glad to have it out in the open, for once not minding that she could read him like a book.

"I don't have time not to be, Oliver. I have a life and I want to call you a friend in it. But if you think I pick and choose my friends according to the amount of money they make, then you don't know me, and I don't have to waste my time proving myself to anyone."

Oliver felt like a whipped dog. It was too plain that she was speaking the truth, that she could take him or leave him at that point as easily as she might accept or reject the tuna salad at the buffet. Suddenly it was imperative that she take him.

He snatched her into his arms and lowered his mouth over hers to shut her up, to keep her from telling him to go away. She resisted with her hands to his chest and angry noises in her throat, but he held on, his hands burning with the feel of silk and cool, soft flesh; his mouth filling with the sweet warmth of her; his mind fogged with the scent of her.

And when her resistance weakened, when her arms went limp about his shoulders and her body grew heavy against his, he held her closer and deepened the kiss.

Never had he needed to rely on a single kiss to make him feel important; to impress a woman; to prove to her that she could hold him near; to beg to be accepted in her life; to convince her that he could contribute to her needs if she'd only give him a chance.

"I'm sorry," he murmured when they stood weak, clinging, and dazed, torn between body and mind, between sex on the spot and returning to the party. "I'm sorry I misjudged you."

"Don't do it again," she said as she desperately tried to gather her wits. "You don't know me."

"I want to."

"I don't like your aunt, but I've tried not to use that ruler on you. You're different. I like you. Please, don't disappoint me," she said, and for a moment it was as if she'd asked him to commit suicide for her. The ultimate test of her faith in him. And for that moment he was completely willing to do it.

It was a simple request. Don't disappoint her. Don't make her sorry that she trusted him. Don't prove her wrong in her hopes that he wasn't like his aunt, who for all her good works was also narrow-minded and a bit of a snob. In an instant, he knew that no matter what the future held for them, he'd spend the rest of his life striving to fulfill her one demand.

"I'll try not to disappoint you," he said. "If you'll answer one question."

"What?" she asked. Her eyes were wide open.

"Are you psychic?"

"Am I what?"

"When I'm angry, I know it's obvious. But how did you know what I was mad about? How did you know about the cream and sugar in my coffee and the Jack Daniels? And what about the weird way you have of knowing what I'm thinking and the—"

"That must be it, then," she said, smiling, his question too impossible to take seriously. "You've found me out. I'm psychic."

"I'm serious."

"I can see that. And I'm confessing. If that makes you feel any better. But we both know I'm not psychic, for crying out loud."

"Then how do you know all those things about me?"

"I don't. I act on hunches and do whatever I think is best."

"Well, it's damned peculiar."

She leaned close, as if to tell him a secret.

"So is life, in case you haven't noticed," she said, locking their arms together. "Come on. I'll show you the work I submitted so you can bid enough money on it to renovate the entire building. Oh. Maybe I should tell you . . ." She put a hand to his shirtfront. He was sure it would leave a permanent impression on his skin. "I have a devout irreverence for money. It's like the world's best joke that so few have so much of it, when so many others need it more. If I give it too much importance, I get a little crazy."

"I'll remember that."

"Good. I didn't want you to think it was personal."

"Of course not," he said, a smile twitching at his lips.

The rest of the evening was perfect. Holly would vanish and then reappear at his side with a smile that let him know where she was happiest.

Her contribution to the auction was an enlarged photograph of a gnarly, work-worn hand cradling the fat, young, innocent hand of a child. It touched the hearts of many a father and son in the crowd and, strangely enough, was taken out of the bidding before the auction began.

"I don't understand how that could happen," she said when she was told by one of her committee chairpersons. "Don't we have rules about things like that?"

"It's the first time anyone's ever offered us that much money to take something out. We didn't know what to do. We've never gotten that much money for anything."

"Well, who was it?"

The woman shrugged. "Gracie didn't say. She said the man came, gave her a big check, and then left her with her mouth hanging open."

"Oliver?" She turned to him. "Can things like this happen? It's not against the law or anything, is it?"

"I don't think so. Not if everyone involved is happy with the purchase price."

"Are we happy, Jannine?"

"We're thrilled," she confided in a low voice.

"Okay," she said pragmatically. "Oliver, have you met Jannine yet? None of this would be possible without her."

Jannine giggled and denied it self-consciously.

"Yes. We met earlier, but she wouldn't tell her phrase," he said, turning Jannine seven shades of scarlet as he examined her head to toe.

Holly empathized. Oliver had a way of looking at a woman that only the most cold-blooded of the sex could ignore. She'd been suffering hot flashes all night because of it and was glad for the respite, sure that Jannine would eventually recover.

If only she were as sure of herself. . . .

How many times had she found herself waiting to feel

his hand at her back as she moved about the room? How many times had she recalled the kiss in the empty corridor and felt her lips tingling? How many times had she been nudged into his side or pressed close to his chest in the crowd and wished for his arms to hold her there?

"I've got it," Oliver said. "The headphone. The K-Y jelly. You're a slick operator."

Jannine grinned. "It was Holly's idea. I couldn't think of anything. I was going to wear my bunny outfit again and call myself a pubic hare, but . . ." She broke off in tongue-tied embarrassment, as she had every time she'd discussed the costume with Holly.

"Holly thought up mine too," he said quickly, coming to her rescue. He turned his head, and Holly was once again in his limelight. "She's very clever, isn't she?"

Jannine agreed that she was, then felt a sudden urge to be needed elsewhere and left.

"You love this stuff, don't you," he asked.

"I like seeing people happy, yes."

"Your patients must love you."

"My patients?"

"The residents at the convalescent center. Do they fight to see who's going to get you for their nurse?"

"I'm not a nurse. I don't even work there. I just volunteer some of my time."

"Oh," he said, taken aback. She'd been so at ease with so many of the people that he'd assumed she was part of the staff. Her efficiency and caring ways had fit the mold of a nurse.

"Nurses come from a special mold, I think." He cringed at her choice of words, but she didn't notice. "They have to care and still be objective, and I can't do that. I'm too impatient. I get angry. I want to see results right away."

"What do you do, then? For a living."

"I work at the Joey Paulson Clinic on Deaver Street. We do crisis intervention, which is a fancy name for a little bit of everything, I guess."

"Like what?"

"Let's see, we find homes for people who've lost theirs. We get food for people who don't have any. We find medical care and psychiatric help for those who need it. We take in runaways and supply prostitutes with prophylactics, and we baby-sit kids while their mothers look for work, and we . . . do a little bit of everything. And if we can't do it, we refer people to places that can."

"You do all this by phone or do people come to you?"

"Both. We do a lot by phone, but they come in too."

The band was interrupted to announce the beginning of the auction, and they continued to talk as they followed the flow of people into the next room.

"Frustrating work," he observed.

"Good work, when it works."

"Is that how you got connected with St. Augustine's, then? Through your work at the clinic?"

"No. Whatever I can do for St. Augustine's is purely personal."

"Don't you ever get depressed?" he asked, knowing that he would.

"Sure I do. But it doesn't do anybody any good to stay that way, now does it?"

No, he supposed it didn't do any good. But to work with the sick and indigent day after day; to live in a rundown apartment building; to have grown up not knowing her real parents . . . Holly Loftin was a woman unlike any he'd known before. An endless fountain of unselfish giving and concern.

She was beautiful, smart, educated. There were people who would do anything in the world for her. Yet there didn't seem to be anything she wanted for herself—except Phil Rosenthal's painting.

"That does it," she exclaimed, when she was outbid once again. "I'm scratching Mrs. Vochec off the guest list."

"The same woman from last year bought Phil's painting?"

"No. She brought her sister-in-law along this year, and *she* got it."

With the main event over, waiters were beginning to clean up the debris, and they were preparing to leave.

"Why didn't you let me raise the bid? I would have been happy to buy—"

"I don't want you to buy me things, Oliver. It isn't necessary."

"I know, but I want to."

"I'd rather you didn't. I'd rather have . . ." she hesitated.

"What?" He waited with eager anticipation.

"I'd rather have a walk in the park, Sunday afternoon," she said. She wanted him to give her things that money couldn't buy. A hug. A kiss. And when she was tired, a shoulder to lean on.

"You got it." He stopped. "Which park?"

"Uh, the one at Lake Merritt. We'll feed the ducks. I work, so it'll have to be about four o'clock. Is that okay?"

"Sure. What if it rains?"

"All the better."

Oliver drove her back to her apartment. She was full of excitement over the success of St. Augustine's Annual Costume Party and Amateur Art Auction—but she wasn't full of herself.

"I'm so pleased for them. They all worked so hard on it," she said, and while he was still musing on her humility, she added, "I can make it from here, Oliver. You don't need to walk up all those stairs. I'll be fine. I'm really glad you came tonight."

"So am I, and I'm walking you up to your door." He was acutely conscious of her all-but-naked state of attire under her coat and could imagine that every pervert within a hundred miles had their antennae up and were aware of it as well. Letting her out at the curb would be analogous to throwing her to the wolves. He opened the car door, and the overhead light came on.

"Oliver, we fought and made up tonight. We laughed and shared stories and talked about our lives. We've covered a lot of territory. But if you come up, I'm going to want you to come in and spend more time with me. You'll want to kiss me and I'll want to let you, and then one thing will lead to another and you'll end up spending the night, and then we'll wake up in the morning wondering if we might not have rushed it a bit and then we'll both feel awkward, and then you might change your mind about the park on Sunday and it'll rain and no one else will be there, and then the ducks'll have to go hungry that day."

"How about just to the front door?" he asked straight-faced, his hand still on the door handle. "I won't go in the building."

"You can watch me from here."

He tipped his head to one side and gauged the distance to the door.

"It won't be easy to kiss you from here."

"Then do it now," she said with an eager smile, her eyes bright and beckoning.

He closed the car door and all but rolled up his sleeves getting ready to kiss her. While she waited patiently, the strangest thing happened. He developed temporary amnesia or something. He couldn't remember which way to tilt his head or where to put his hands.

He adjusted his weight to free the tail of his jacket, put one arm over the back of the seat, and looped the other loosely around her waist.

Yes. Yes. It was coming back to him, he thought in a wash of relief as he moved in for the kill. He felt her breath on his lips, they parted. His eyes began to close. He brushed her lips, she turned her head. He planted a big one on her cheek.

Playful and quick, she came around to return his peck and sat back grinning.

"Good night, Oliver."

"Good night, Holly," he said, working hard not to smile back. This wasn't the sort of behavior he wanted to encourage.

She wouldn't have gotten out of the car if she hadn't heard the amusement in his voice. As it was, she walked to her door reaffirming her belief that he wanted more from her than what he could get from at least two hundred other women in the Bay Area.

Her phone rang ten minutes later.

"It's three A.M. . . . that makes it the next morning,

and I don't feel the least bit awkward about spending the night with you," he said, the line crackling a bit.

"Good," she said, laughing, checking the window to see if he was still parked in front of her building. "Where are you?"

"Halfway across the bridge. But I can turn around and come back if you want me to."

"Don't tempt me, Oliver. It's not nice to tempt a lady."

"Who says I'm nice?"

"I do. I'll see you Sunday afternoon."

There was a brief silence. "Good night, Holly. I had a good time."

"Me too. Good night, Oliver."

He was nice. And gentle and sweet and tolerant—tolerant as hell, if the tension he felt was anywhere near what she was feeling.

FIVE

Tension wasn't exactly what Oliver was feeling. Tension was what you felt during a business merger. Tension came when the shares were down before a stockholders' meeting. Tension didn't keep him awake all night or make his food taste like a mouthful of dust. Tension didn't keep him reaching for the phone or blur the words in his magazines. It didn't make him restless and it didn't cause him to stare off into space like a zombie.

Holly wasn't making him tense, she was making him crazy.

"Have you ever heard of a place called St. Augustine's?" he asked his aunt the next day over a light lunch. "It's a convalescent home. In Oakland?"

They shared the Carey House estate as a matter of convenience. To try to dislodge his aunt would have been very inconvenient for Oliver—strenuous, aggravating, and more trouble than he cared to undertake. Besides, he knew little or nothing about the running of a large household, though he often suspected that it could pretty much run itself. The place was too big to live in alone anyway. And to hide away or avoid a bash for the cause of the week, he could always use the apartment downtown.

It was a greater convenience to Elizabeth Carey George, however, to live in her childhood home and not have to explain to anyone why her husband's lack of good investments and surplus of expensive mistresses had left her with little more than another fine old San Francisco name to attach to her own, and a heart full of bitterness.

All in all, it was a fairly amicable arrangement.

"It doesn't ring a bell, dear," she said, looking up from the promotional material she was reviewing for her newest crusade—to save the South American limpkin that would soon see extinction with the destruction of the rain forest. "Why do you ask?"

"Just curious. What about the Joey Paulson Clinic?"

"Paulson. Paulson. There's something familiar about the name, but I might be thinking of the Palm Beach Paulsons. I heard last night that Barry's been cheating on her with some showgirl he met in Vegas. Can you imagine it? And Tiffany is a Brooks, and you know how they stick together. He'll be lucky to get out of that marriage with a spare shirt."

"He should be grateful for that," he said, a woman-lover himself but not without a certain amount of restraint and decorum. He liked to think of himself as a man of principle and self-control. Women were a matter of self-discipline, and he had little respect for a man who had none.

"What is this sudden interest in Oakland, dear? I understand the land values aren't worth investing in, and they say . . ."

"No, it's not about business. I . . . I was talking to Phil Rosenthal last night, and he thought there might be a couple of places over there that could use some help from the foundation."

"The Carey Foundation, as you well know, is overextended as it is. I'm firmly committed to asking the trustees to reevaluate several of our grants at the next meeting. We can't possibly take on anyone new at this time."

"But we can take on some stupid birds in South America?" he asked, vexed that when he'd finally found a worthy cause of his own, the funds in the foundation he'd been managing most of his adult life were already allocated elsewhere.

"Don't be silly, dear, you know as well as I do that we can't use the foundation money on anything but people-related concerns. You don't remember grandfather Edgar, of course, but he was adamant on the point. I think it had something to do with the time the dogcatcher came through and picked up three of his dogs and put them to sleep before he could bail them out. He was furious about that for years."

"So how are you supporting your birds?"

"Oh, this is another group entirely, dear. I'm helping Marsha Levenson with this one, you know how she is. . . ."

She went on to tell him in detail, but he only half listened. Hell, he didn't need a damned foundation to support the Paulson Clinic. He could do it himself. If they had more money, they could pay better wages and Holly could move to a nicer neighborhood . . . unless they spent the money on food and medical care.

He was beginning to see that there was more to being charitable than simply writing a check.

While Oliver had inherited the greater portion of his wealth, Holly had to work for hers. And while most of the Carey legacy was tied up in banking, Holly hated banks with a passion.

Stopping for the mail she'd forgotten to pick up the day before, she pulled another overdrawn notice from her mailbox—her third in a week—and fought a sick, smothering feeling as she climbed the stairs to her apartment.

Money. Why was it always money?

She put the key in the lock and smiled as she recalled the art auction and the way she had kept raising Lena Vochec's bid and glancing at her with a too-sweet smile to get her to top it. It was a good thing Lena hated to lose. It would have been terribly embarrassing to have to admit to several hundred people that her savings account was in even worse shape than her checking account. It had no shape at all, in fact.

Well, she'd been bluffing people like Lena Vochec for years. Loan officers. Bank officials. Foundation directors. And she was good at it. No sense giving up something she excelled at just because it was a little dishonest, she thought, tossing the overdrawn notice into a drawer with the others.

It was only money, after all, and there was no point in letting it get to her, when she'd be walking in the park with an eat-'em-alive hunk of a man in less than an hour. She smiled. It had started to rain already.

Weekends were long anyway. People who were out looking for work during the week brought all their problems to the clinic on Saturday—and stood in line till Sunday, it seemed. But this had been an especially long two days for her.

Oliver had been on her mind like a brain tumor. The sound of his laughter, the sudden catch in his voice, the tiny crescent-shaped scar on the back of his hand . . .

There was a knock at her door.

"You know, you're pretty creepy yourself," she said, pulling the door open without checking to see who it was first, knowing as well as she knew her own face that he'd be standing there. "I was just thinking about you."

"You were?" He was pleased. Well, more than pleased. He wanted to rip her clothes off and bury himself so deep inside her that parts of him would never know daylight again.

"I was wondering if you'd bring an umbrella."

"Oh. No. I didn't even think about it," he said, at a loss. "I guess I should have. We can stop someplace and buy one."

"Absolutely not. Why go to the park when you know it's going to rain, just to stand under an umbrella?"

Why go at all? he wanted to know, but didn't ask. He'd been so eager to see her, he'd arrived thirty minutes early. Another first. Maybe she wouldn't notice.

They teetered in the doorway, wanting to kiss hello, wondering if they should shake hands, deciding it might be best to delay any physical contact.

"Come in and sit for a minute," she said. "I want to change clothes."

Why? he wondered. She'd be soaked to the bone in five minutes.

Her apartment seemed to have shrunk since his last visit. He could spit from one end to the other. It was wallpapered, had freshly painted trim, and was neat and cheery, but it gave "efficiency apartment" new meaning. She could cook breakfast, brush her teeth, and make the bed in three easy steps. And why hadn't he noticed before that there was no bedroom, he speculated, pondering the couch, trusting it would fold out into a bed. A one-room apartment with a kitchen and bath. Oakland wasn't any different than any other town. There were places to live, and then there were places to live . . . but this wasn't one of them.

Holly, on the other hand, didn't think of it as all *that* terrible a place. She knew most everyone in her building and was on saluting terms with several of the merchants and a few of the people across the street. She liked to call it a neighborhood with potential—for both harmony and discord.

"I'm glad you came early," she called from the bathroom. He rolled his eyes. She'd noticed. "I've been dying to ask if you really asked Clare Hilendorfer if her costume the other night was a bun in the oven?"

He grimaced.

"Well, she was standing there with those cooking mitt things on both hands and she did look pregnant. I didn't see the little handle she was holding until it was too late."

"And by then she really was too hot to handle, huh?" she asked, stepping back into the room, grinning.

"She was . . . upset. I apologized, but the damage was done."

"She almost laughed about it yesterday."

"You went to St. Augustine's yesterday? I thought you had to work yesterday."

"I did go to work. The hospital's on my way home, so I stop in to visit a lot. Thursdays I'm there all day. Are you ready to go?"

The weather in Oakland was remarkably different from that of San Francisco in the summertime. Warmer, drier, no fog. In winter the differences were less noticeable—they were both a little cooler and wetter.

Holly had put on a bulky knit sweater and blue jeans that reminded Oliver of the wallpaper in her apartment —old, clean, and stuck tight to the walls. She had one of those rear ends that were almost impossible not to reach out and smack.

"Ow," she cried, startled, rubbing her tush as she turned to him. "What was that for?"

"It was a vote of understanding for Barry Paulson," he said, looking straight ahead into the rain as he passed her on the sidewalk.

"Who's Barry Paulson?"

"A man with two shirts and no self-control," he answered cryptically, hoping that poor Barry was giving up everything he owned for a fanny as nice as Holly's. He stepped to the curb to open the door of his car. "I have absolutely no respect for him."

She was frowning at him in confusion, then noticed the open door.

"Oh, no. We'll ruin your upholstery with our wet

clothes. There's a BART station two blocks down, and it'll take us right to the park."

He looked up and down the street in both directions and saw plenty of other cars. But in their midst his late-model Lincoln looked like a shiny invitation to grand theft auto. Why hadn't he brought his driver?

"Okay," he said with misgivings. He snatched a brown paper bag from the front seat. He locked the doors and set the alarm.

Strange . . . When she sidled up to him, slipping her hand into his, he didn't once look back at his car.

"Isn't this great?" she asked, tipping her face to the downpour. It was running down his raincoat in streamlets. His hair was plastered to his head, his face was wet, and he had to keep blinking to see. It was pretty great all right. But only because the raindrops sparkled in her eyelashes and lingered dewy-fresh on her skin, calling him to sip away every drop to quench his thirst. She pushed her dark hair up and away from her face. He wondered if he'd ever known anything as uniquely and naturally beautiful as Holly Loftin. "There's nothing like a good rain to wash away your troubles," she said.

"Do you have troubles?"

"Who, me?" she asked, thinking of her drawer full of bills and overdrawn bank slips. "Troubles are for people who think too much, but never think to change anything."

They talked about Oakland on the way to the park—after a small show of getting him his own transit pass.

"After school I took some time off; there were . . ." she hesitated briefly ". . . some things I'd been wanting to do for a long time. I started looking around San Francisco, and then I got sidetracked to Oakland. I found someone here that I didn't think I could leave. So I stayed. I got a job and a place to live and started a life here. And I like it. I like the town and I like the people. I'm comfortable here."

Only a fool would have assumed that there hadn't been any other men in her life—and Oliver was no fool. He wasn't even disappointed. But he felt a certain blackness in his heart for the person who'd had the power to make her give up her home and family to live in a strange town, alone, fending for herself.

"Have you been anywhere else?" he asked. "Have you done much traveling?"

The answer was no, and the rest of the trip was taken up with places she dreamed of seeing and the places he'd already seen.

The rain drizzled as they ambled through the children's park and the picnic area and stood on the banks of the lake watching a few die-hard sailors braving the wind and waves. Their conversation bounced from hither to thither, but nowhere near yawn. They laughed and teased and fed whole wheat bread from his brown paper bag to the squawking mallards and a few wayward Canadian honkers.

"I wasn't sure if they'd prefer white or dark bread. So I brought both," he explained.

"Let's keep 'em healthy and feed them the dark. What are you going to do with the other loaf?"

He shrugged. He hadn't thought about it. Throw it away? Leave it on a bench for someone else to feed to the ducks?

"Can I have it?"

"Sure," he said, handing her the bag, concern biting at his mind. Couldn't she afford food?

"The Paulson Clinic thanks you," she said with a gracious smile. "Even leftover duck food is a welcome sight."

Suddenly he was feeling too fat, too well fed.

"I wish it were a truckload of bread."

"So do I."

The best part of the afternoon, however, were the long, contented moments of silence. Whole segments of time when being male or female, rich or poor, blue blood or foster child didn't matter. Precious pieces of time when it was enough to simply be and be together.

It was during one such moment when Holly chanced to glance at Oliver. She liked looking at him. He was certainly handsome, but it was his confidence and quiet intelligence that appealed to her most. It made her feel safe.

There wasn't a woman alive, or a man for that matter, who didn't want to feel that the person they were with was capable of protecting them, of taking care of them, of caring for them. Being the captain of one's own ship was frightening and lonely sometimes. A safe harbor and solid land were always a comforting sight. Oliver was a comforting sight.

He was feeling safe and comfortable, too, she noted. It made her happy and sad at once to see that he felt free to be himself in her presence, that he didn't think he needed to be constantly in good cheer for her. But it was a shame to see that he had that isolated and lonely look on his face again, the one he got when his guard was down; when he didn't think anyone would notice; when he didn't think anyone would care.

"What was he like?" she asked softly.

He chuckled and shook his head. When he looked at her, his expression had changed to one of futile acceptance.

"He was a good man," he said, not bothering to pretend that he didn't know who she was asking about. Obviously, she'd been diddling with his thoughts again. "Born in the wrong century, but a good man."

"What was he like?" she asked again.

"He wrote poetry," he said, sounding almost as if he didn't approve of it. He turned and walked slowly along the shore, away from the ducks and geese. "He wore a bow tie every day for as long as I knew him, and he never once raised his voice to me."

Holly's brows rose. At first she thought these were strange things to recall about a loved one. Stranger still, that Oliver didn't sound as if they were cherished memories. But then she remembered Marie's husband, Roberto, and smiled. He always wore long-sleeved white shirts and rolled the cuffs up to his elbows. And when he spoke, his voice could be heard in every corner of the big old house on Chambrey Street.

"What sort of poetry did he write?" she asked, thinking it a good place to start. Oliver needed to talk about his father. It didn't really matter about what, he simply needed to get started.

"Crap mostly," he said, surprising her. "Stuff about loyalty and truth and loving a son and springtime and fulfilling your own destiny."

"Oliver?" she broke in, unable to connect the hostility in his voice with the grief in his eyes.

"I hated that stuff," he went on. "I used to think he was the biggest wimp that ever walked the earth. A sissy. And he was old. Close to fifty when I was born. I used to think it was because he was so weird that no woman would marry him before he met my mother, and that she had been duped, tricked somehow into having his child. Later I was a little more cynical about it. I figured that it probably took him fifty years to figure out how to get it up."

His mouth closed on his bitterness, forming a slim, angry line. He stopped and looked out over the lake. She watched his chest heave with heated emotions. He was silent for a few minutes. She wasn't sure of what to say or do and took her cue from him. Finally his lids lowered over his eyes, as if blocking out some terrible scene, and then he looked at her as if he'd forgotten she was there.

"He wasn't around much when I was young. He was there but not around. He was like this kindly old gentleman who lived with us. Gentle, quiet, off in a world of his own. I didn't know what he did all day when he went off to the office. I didn't know what he did all evening in his study. He never offered to share his life with me, and I didn't care enough to ask." He started walking again. "My uncle Max turned up at a pivotal time in my life. I was almost eight and my mother had recently died and . . . I guess I was sort of lost." He looked down at his shoes. "Soft things and nice smells always make me think of her, but I don't really remember much about her," he said as an aside. "Anyway, Max George had married Elizabeth a few years earlier, and when I might have turned to the kindly old gentleman who was my father for comfort and companionship, Max showed up. He and Elizabeth moved in with us. Johanna came, too, but she was away at school most of the time. At the time, I thought they came to live with us because my father didn't want to have to take care of me, but I later found out it was because they were broke and had nowhere else to go. And it never occurred to me that I could have been sent away to school like Johanna if my father had wanted me out of his hair."

She slid her hand between his arm and body. Instinctively he quickly took her fingers in his and held them tight.

"Max was a real character. He liked to watch football, baseball, horse racing, hockey, anything he could bet on. But I didn't see any of the betting going on. All I saw was him taking the time to take me with him. I thought he was the best thing to come along since skateboards. He was loud and happy and he didn't care how late he kept me out at night. Not like the old man. All he cared about was my getting my homework done and making sure Max got me home early so I'd get plenty of sleep. The few times he'd remember to show up at my soccer games or pick me up from football practice, I'd want to slither under the sod. He embarrassed me to death. The world's oldest and most boring father, and he was all mine."

"You were young, Oliver. All boys want Superman to be their dad," she said, finally realizing that the contempt in his manner was not for his father but for himself.

"Max was Superman," he told her. "He introduced me to the wild, wonderful world of women when I was fifteen. I'd look at him and then I'd look at me and then

I'd look at my father and . . . I didn't even try to hide my disgust for him after that," he said, his shame heavy in his heart. "I was so blind."

She couldn't stand to watch him beating himself up for deeds long in the past.

"When did it all change?" she asked. "When did you fall in love with your father?"

Her wording jolted him. Technically, however, falling in love with his father and out of love with Max was pretty much what had happened. He smiled and sighed, his memory fast-forwarding to a more pleasant time.

"It started in my second year of college. I was prelaw at USC Berkeley. I could have stayed on campus, but I actually had more freedom staying at home. The old man had long since stopped trying to make any attempts at fathering me, and nobody else gave a damn what I did. I was out of control," he said, having no trouble with the admission. "Fighting, drinking, sleeping around. I had money and freedom and a will of my own. A dangerous combination for a kid as stupid as I was."

"For any kid, I would think," she said, amazed at how hard he was being on himself. Times had changed and turned out for the best, but Oliver hadn't put any of it into perspective yet.

"I was accused of cheating on my finals," he announced. It sounded an awful lot like he'd been accused of murder. "They could have accused me of just about anything else in those days, and I probably would have been guilty, but . . . I never could bring myself to cheat —on girls, or tests, or anything else. And for the first time in a very long time, I was scared. I'd had minor run-ins with the law that hadn't scared me that much."

"They could have expelled you, ruined your career," she said, fully understanding the implications.

"So what if they did?" He laughed. "If I never worked a day in my life, I'd have had plenty of money, and I knew it. And when the old man died, I'd have had more."

"Then why did you care? What difference would it have made? You could have gone to fifty other schools that were just as good, graduated, and gone on to law school. Why was going to USC so important?"

"It wasn't."

"Then what was it?"

"I couldn't get anyone to believe that I hadn't cheated. No one believed me. No one believed *in* me. I was like this invisible thing that no one could see or hear or take seriously. No one cared."

"Except your father."

He nodded. "I went to Max first, of course. By then I'd discovered he wasn't the superman I'd believed him to be. He was forever playing around behind Elizabeth's back, and every loan shark in town had his private number. But he knew stuff. He could wiggle out of anything. I'd seen him do it a hundred times over."

"What did he tell you to do?"

"He told me to lie. He told me to tell them I didn't do it, that they couldn't prove I did it, and if they expelled me, I'd sue."

"But . . ."

"I know." He laughed again. "I was innocent. I told him I was. But even he didn't believe me."

"So you went to your father."

He shook his head. "What could he do? He was a wimp, remember?"

"What did you do?"

"I demanded a review board hearing. I was going to defend myself—but I didn't stand a chance. There wasn't a professor at that school who was willing to give me the benefit of the doubt, or one I hadn't insulted yet either, it seemed. There wasn't even a glimmer of a second chance in the room when I walked in that day."

"What happened?"

"I stated my case and they pretended to listen. They conferred for about half a second and came back to me with blood in the eyes. Then, just as they started to read me the riot act, the door in the back of the room opened. I'll never forget it. Everyone turned to look and there was this little old man standing there, wearing a red bow tie and, holding in his hand this dumb hat he always wore. I thought I was going to sink through the floor. It even crossed my mind to pretend that I didn't know who he was, but then he started talking, real soft the way he always did, so people had to stop breathing to hear what he was saying."

He was lost in the recollection for a moment, then he smiled.

"He said he was ashamed to have to admit that I was his son, but nevertheless the fact was inescapable—that was the way he talked, like a Victorian throwback. He said that I had very little character, that I was irresponsible, spoiled, and selfish, but that, as was true of even the lowest of the lowly, I did have a redeeming quality." He laughed heartily. "He had those profs sitting on the edge of their chairs, wondering what it was."

"And . . ." she prompted, failing to see any humor.

"He told them that I was so greedy and self-serving that I always took whatever I wanted, that I didn't know how to cheat because I'd never had to. And he knew for a fact that I never lied because I didn't have enough self-respect to care what anyone thought of me. And, therefore—that's what he said, "therefore"—I couldn't have cheated on my exams because I wouldn't bother to lie about it if I had. Then he proposed that they let me repeat the exam under close observation to prove that I knew the material."

"And did you?"

"Yes, but I was so nervous, I wasn't sure I'd remember any of it for the exam."

"And did you talk to your father afterward?"

"I asked him why he did it, why he came to my defense." He paused. "He said he did it for my mother. That what little goodness there was in me, was left there by her. And because he loved her, he would always love the goodness in me."

"It doesn't sound as if there was much there to love, Oliver."

He chuckled. "There wasn't. But after that I started seeing things differently. Not right away. But gradually. It bothered me that the only person in the world who believed in me, who believed there was at least one shred of good in me somewhere, was this shriveled-up old man who wrote poetry. It fascinated me. I wanted to know why. I wanted to know what it was in him that made him believe in me after all I'd done to him."

"And did you ever find out?"

"Oh, sure. But it took me another ten years."

"Ten years?"

"When he retired eight years ago and moved to Palm Springs—for the drier climate—he turned everything over to me. I'd changed some by then." He chuckled. "I was still a crazy kid inside, but I worked hard at controlling it. I thought I was as straight as a wall. I wanted to be. I wanted . . . not to disappoint the old man. I didn't want him to know how wrong he was about me. But that didn't happen overnight, and trustees and board members have very long memories, and, well, my father was going to be a hard act for anyone to follow."

"They all liked him."

He nodded. "I worked for him for a while when I got out of school and was humbled every time I rediscovered the fact that his quiet thoughtfulness extended far beyond his poetry to a very cunning business mind. He was a genius. Very clever. Made a ton of money for the company and the foundation and never took any credit for it. It . . . hurt when the board and the trustees refused my nomination. I knew I wouldn't ever be able to fill his shoes, but I'd been trying to emulate him some—his honesty, his respect and genuine concern for other people . . . his kindness, gentleness. . . ."

"But everyone still thought you were a spoiled brat," she concluded.

"Pretty much."

"So, what happened?"

"He called a meeting. I was conveniently out of town at the time, but I've heard that he reminded everyone that it was he who had made them all rich, and that doing so had been a mere by-product of his true intent. He was Adrian Carey and he was the boss. He hadn't been working for them all those years, and if they couldn't accept the son that he trusted and loved and had been building the company for as a legacy of that love, then he'd tear it apart and sell it piece by piece before he died, and they all knew there wouldn't be a damned thing they could do to stop him. It was the first time anyone had ever heard him yell or swear."

Holly had goose bumps racing up her arms. She wanted him to start over at the beginning and tell the story again.

"I went running down to Palm Springs for his advice a lot those first few years," he remembered good-naturedly. "And he never failed me. Never had failed me, really. He'd always been there, he just . . . well, it just took me a long time to get to know him."

"And now you miss him."

"Like an arm or a leg. I feel as if there's a big chunk of me missing."

"If your father could see that the good in you was left by your mother, then what honesty and intelligence and gentleness and kindness you have was left by him. And as long as you are all those things, then he isn't really gone, is he?" she asked, almost as if she were talking to herself. She was even more speculative when she added, "Maybe that's why people have children."

They passed back into a companionable silence, comfortable in their own thoughts, content to share time and space.

The space Oliver was sharing, however, was somehow broader, augmented in a way that had him breathing more deeply and curbing an urge to stretch his muscles. He felt as if a great weight had been lifted from his chest, or a dark cloud that had settled in his heart had suddenly dissipated. He recalled many forgotten memories of his father with gladness and knew not a single pang of guilt or pain.

"Know what I feel like doing?" he asked abruptly.

"Buying ice cream?" she asked hopefully, her eyes fixed on the Double Dip Cafe across the street from the park. There was an ice cream Christmas tree, with all fifty-six flavors, painted on the window.

"I wish you'd stop that. It makes me nervous as hell."

"What?"

"You know what."

She grinned. "Can I help it if I was thinking how romantic it would be if you were to buy me an ice cream cone to eat in the rain a week before Christmas?"

"Most women wouldn't be thinking that was romantic," he grumbled. "They'd be thinking I was trying to freeze them to death. And, Ms. Knowitall, *I* was actually thinking I'd like to get in out of the rain. This isn't my idea of a romantic date."

"It isn't?" She looked surprised. "Are you telling me that you don't think kissing in the rain is romantic?"

"We aren't kissing."

"We could be."

He stopped walking and turned to her, holding his breath.

"Could we be?"

She smiled and gave him an all-things-are-possible look.

SIX

No one would have guessed that he was trembling inside when he palmed her cheek in one big hand. No one would have guessed how often he'd relived their first kiss or how much he'd looked forward to the next. No one would have guessed that the drops of water he thumbed from her lips were as silky and warm as her skin or that her eyes could sparkle like gold dust. No one would have guessed that her hand could sear his skin through a coat and a sweater or how crippling it could be to watch her lips part in anticipation. No one would have guessed . . .

Oliver bent his head. He watched her pupils dilate as he came closer, and her eyes close as he brushed his lips against hers. Tender and tantalizing. He traced them with the tip of his tongue. Dewy fresh. Honey sweet. He nibbled on her lower lip. Supple and sensuous. He pulled her tight into his arms. It felt so right, so real. His jagged nerves snapped at the tiny sound in her throat when his mouth covered hers and he fed. Hungry, greedy, and possessive.

No one would have guessed . . .

She wrapped her arms about his neck and hung on tight. The earth had slipped from beneath her feet, and the cloudy skies grew dim and fanciful. There were stars and then clouds and then nothing at all. Nothing but the pounding of her heart and a clawing need. Her skin screamed for his touch; her muscles ached with restraint. Joints grew weak, and passion spread like water over glass.

Attack and surrender, her body played games and her senses were unreliable. She was strong and weak at once, starving but too feeble to eat.

They separated in a fog that was thicker and more profoundly mysterious than any misty cloud that had ever covered the Bay Area.

He stepped back, but didn't release her. She was hardly breathing. Her soul wept with deprivation. She opened her eyes to see the wonder and the struggle in his eyes, and knew that they mirrored her own.

He smiled, thinking how strange it must look with the rain turning to steam all around them.

"Maybe we should try that ice cream after all," he said.

She laughed. "Maybe they'll let us roll in it."

He had a sudden vision of the last two tattered shirts in his closet and couldn't have cared less—he kissed her again for the sheer pleasure of it and knew a sudden and deep empathy for poor Barry Paulson.

———◆———◆———

"So, what exactly is your idea of a romantic date?" she asked, licking ice cream from the corner of her mouth with the tip of her tongue in a way that had him licking his own chops—but for a very different reason.

A romantic date . . . Dating was dating. The groundwork for sex. The mandatory price one paid for respectable sex, he supposed. But a romantic date? Certainly, sex would be an element to consider, but somehow he wanted romance to be more than that for Holly. More for him too. He wanted it to be sex without touching; a kiss in every glance; whispering secrets and sharing dreams without speaking. . . . A romantic date wouldn't be easy to arrange.

"Do you like the theater?" he asked, opting for old standbys, hoping for the best.

"Which one?"

"Which one?"

"Well, I like the one on Bow Street better than I like the ones downtown," she said, unable to resist the urge to tease him. "It's still a big screen and it's really old-fashioned, but they have great popcorn. But then there are so many theaters to choose from that I suppose it would depend on which movie we wanted to see."

"No. I meant the *theater* theater. You know, plays and . . ."

"Oh," she said. "You want to do that stuck-up stuff."

"Stuck-up stuff?"

"Where people get all dressed up to show off their new clothes before they sit and watch some sad old story that people used to watch wearing bed sheets."

He turned to her in utter disbelief—and that's when he saw the merry twinkle in her eyes.

"Exactly."

She chuckled and tossed the napkin and bottom of her cone into a trash can as they passed by.

"Stuck-up stuff can be romantic sometimes," she conceded airily. "I wouldn't mind seeing a play, but not the opera."

"You don't like opera?"

"I grew up with Italians. I love opera," she said, taking his hand and turning it a bit. "You're dripping over here." She licked up a little of his triple Dutch chocolate, saying, "But they're doing *Rusalka* at the opera house, and I hate it when the prince dies. It's probably true that the sad ones have all the prettiest music, but I prefer the comedies. I see enough tragedy. I hear the Joffrey Ballet is coming next season, and I wouldn't mind seeing them again, no matter what they're performing."

Chocolate ice cream dribbled between his fingers as his mind raced. She liked opera and ballet! Most of his dates tolerated it for a variety of reasons—to show off their clothes, as Holly had said; to say they'd been; to be with him. But it was a rare woman in his experience who knew anything about it or showed real appreciation for it.

His love of music was a gift from his father, one of the few interests they'd been able to share. He actually preferred symphony music to opera and ballet, but common ground was common ground, and it was hard to come by in this particular area. He wouldn't split hairs.

"If I can find a good comedy playing someplace, would you like to go?" he asked, grateful to see another trash can in their path.

"Wellll," she said, sly and designing and not trying to hide it. "If you really want to go to all that trouble to impress me, and if you really want to be romantic, they're doing Debussy at Davies Symphony Hall."

"You like Debussy?"

"Doesn't everyone? They're doing *La Mer* and *En blanc et noir*, I heard, for sure. But maybe they'll do a few other preludes. *Children's Corner* or *Estampes*. If they do *Claire de lune*, I'll cry. I love his piano pieces."

She chatted and walked on as he came to a gradual stop beside the trash can, staring at her, cold chills running up his spine that had nothing to do with the weather. The mostly eaten ice cream cone fell from his fingers as he realized that she'd plucked nearly every word she'd said directly from his heart.

"What?" she asked, turning back when she discovered he was missing, only to catch him staring at her as if she were some foreign creature he'd never seen before. "Is something wrong?"

"No," he said, shaking his head clear. "I was just thinking that I have recordings of *L'Isle Joyeuse* and *Iberia* that you might like. They're . . . not done that often."

"I'd love to," she said, watching him. He examined his sticky fingers in disgust and finally bent to rinse them in a fairly clean puddle of rainwater on the sidewalk. He dried them with his handkerchief and then held out his hand to her. She took it, saying, "I've heard *Iberia*, but not *L'Isle*. Is it as pretty as the others?"

While he expounded on Debussy's movements, she was regarding the strength and heat of his hand. Solid and comforting. To be sexually attracted to a man was something, but to like him, truly like him, was something even more special and rare. She'd seen him four times, and yet sometimes she felt as if she'd known him forever. She had to keep swallowing the urge to ask him, *Where the hell have you been?* As if he'd been away too long. And still he was new and constantly refreshing.

Oliver had the potential to be everything he had been in his past, what his aunt and Barbara Renbrook were now. A snob. But his ego was strong enough to be teased, he could be spontaneous, he could do a tolerable job of walking in the rain, and he wasn't too proud to wash his hands in rainwater.

Rich or poor, she believed that people were born to certain stations in life and that it took a great deal of courage, love, and understanding to overcome them. Oliver knew and understood these things. He was a man among men, capable of great things—capable of one great thing in particular, making her fall in love.

It was nearly nine by the time they'd finished eating at the little cafe a few blocks from her apartment. The rain had stopped, but everything had looked coated in glass as they'd walked home.

"So, Holly," he said, as his lips played over hers outside her apartment door. "We've fed the ducks. Will anyone go hungry tomorrow if you invite me in tonight?"

At present she didn't care if the whole world starved to death. . . . But it was a terrible thought.

"No. No one will starve tomorrow because of us . . ." he kissed her till her toes curled, ". . . and you're welcome to come in . . ." a scattering of sweet sipping kisses down her neck, ". . . you can even stay the night, but . . ."

"But?" He pulled back to look at her.

Her sigh was long and hard and disappointed.

"I won't be here."

"Why not? Where are you going?"

"It's my turn to work the turnaround. I have to go back to work tonight."

"But you worked all day."

"We're short staffed. Weekends especially. We take turns on the night shift, and on weekends we do turn-arounds. Eight on, eight off, turn around and do it over again."

"When the hell are you supposed to sleep?"

"Oh." She grinned. "Were you planning to actually sleep here tonight?"

"I'm serious. Doesn't that place ever close?"

She didn't like the tone of his voice, but she understood it.

"People don't stop having problems between five P.M. and nine the next morning. In fact, it's the dark hours that are most frightening for them." She put her hand deep into the pocket of her jeans and withdrew the key to her apartment. She turned to the door, saying, "Darkness can be very heavy. Overwhelming sometimes. Despair sets in fast without the light of hope. Nothing happens at night. While the rest of the world sleeps, the hopeless are awake, thinking and worrying and deciding they're better off dead."

"I'm sorry," he said, not immune to the plight of the poor, but more concerned for Holly's well-being. He followed her inside. "But isn't there some other way to arrange the schedule? You need to sleep. When are you . . ."

She laughed at his guilty expression when he realized she would have been sleeping if she hadn't been out with him. She reached up on tiptoe to kiss him.

"Today with you and the rain was better than twenty-four hours of sleep. I had a wonderful time." She held her arms out at her sides. "I feel happy and full of energy and ready to take on the world."

Damned if she didn't look it, too, he thought.

"When do you have to go back?" he asked, slipping his arms around her waist, a move that came as naturally as blinking.

"Eleven."

He wanted to drive her to work, to spend every second he could with her, but he knew she'd need her car to get back in the morning.

"Will you call me when you get home tomorrow?"

"Are you up at eight?" She grinned.

"I will be tomorrow." He kissed the smirk off her face and waited till he felt her knees buckle before he lifted his face from hers. "Clavin'll wake me up."

"Who's Clavin? The butler?" She was being facetious, but when he smirked at her . . . "You really have one, don't you? And maids, too, I bet." She shook her head. "I keep forgetting."

"I know. And I like it. But you really should develop some respect for money, you know. It can buy more than bread."

"It can't buy anything important."

"True. But it can make life a little easier so you can enjoy the important things."

That was true, too, though she wished it weren't. There was such a vast and vexing void between what was and what ought to be that she simply couldn't reconcile herself to it. Life should be easy for everyone. Not opulently easy, necessarily, but basically easy. If one was blessed with a child, none of that joy should be tarnished with concerns for keeping it warm and fed and safe. If one was lucky enough to fall in love, none of the thrill should be discolored with fears of keeping each other healthy, sheltered, and out of harm's way. It simply wasn't right.

"You'd better go. Clavin'll be worried about you," she said, pressing her cheek to his chest and holding on tight as she banished the evil thoughts she had for his money. It wasn't his fault he was rich, any more than it was her fault that she knew so many frightened and hungry people.

He could almost feel her trying to bridge the gap that had formed between them, that enormous hollow of money. The smell of the rain and her clean, fresh hair filled his head, and he knew in that instant that he'd give it all away to make her happy in his arms.

A staggering thought, that. To give up everything for her. For Holly. Was that love? Or some outrageous form of lust? She felt so good, so close, so right, but . . .

"I agree with you. If I don't leave now, I'll be here in the morning when you get back."

"I wouldn't mind that," she said, feeling a bit lost when he held her away from him.

"You'll be tired in the morning, an easy target."

She grinned.

"I'm an easy target now, in case you hadn't noticed," she said, stepping into his embrace.

He laughed softly, pressing a kiss to her temple. Just like that, they were together again, on a sturdy bridge so far above the money that it couldn't be seen anymore.

"I noticed. But there's not enough time for me to do anything about it."

"There's still time. How much do you need?"

"Lots." He kissed her long and leisurely, a promise of things to come. "Possibly all night." He kissed her again. "Three or four days perhaps."

A lifetime, he thought. Maybe more.

"Clavin, have there been any calls for me?" It was nine o'clock and he'd been up since seven-thirty waiting to hear from Holly.

He'd listened sharply during the ten minutes it had taken him to shower. But he still could have missed it. Come to think of it, there was more than one line in the house. She'd said she'd called the house before, but maybe he should have given her his private number.

"No, sir, no calls," Clavin said.

Tall, thin, and half-bald, and more like family to Oliver than several of his blood relatives, Clavin poured coffee from a shiny silver pot into a thin china cup and set it in front of his young employer. With every crease of his livery unwrinkled, he then stepped aside.

"If a woman named Holly Loftin calls, I'll take it immediately."

"Very well."

He opened the newspaper and picked at his customary breakfast of fresh fruit and dry toast and missed Clavin's hesitation.

"Sir. I believe there's been a misunderstanding."

"About what?" he asked absently, his mind on Holly. What if she'd been mugged last night? What if someone had broken into the apartment. . . . Hell, they could have blown the damned door in. . . . What if . . . ?

"About Ms. Loftin."

"What about her?"

"When she started calling—"

"When she started calling? How many times has she called?"

"She called several times a while back, after Mister Adrian passed on. And then again this morning."

"Why wasn't I told?" He recalled her saying that she'd called but hadn't been able to get through to him. "I asked you five seconds ago if I'd had any calls, and you said no."

"I beg your pardon, but I was under the impression that you weren't taking Ms. Loftin's calls."

"When the hell did I tell you that?" he shouted, his anger rising so fast and so uncontrollably that it brought him to his feet.

"You didn't, sir," he said, falling back on his "sirs" when faced with Oliver's rage. "Miss Renbrook—"

"Miss Renbrook. Babs? Barbara," he added, recalling her preferred title. "What the bloody hell does she have to do with this?"

"Sir, after Mister Adrian . . . passed away . . . sir, I left Ms. Loftin's messages on the table with the others. Ms. Renbrook was going to return a few of them for you, I believe, when she came across those from Ms. Loftin.

She told me not to take any more, as you wouldn't appreciate getting them." Clavin looked at him nervously. Oliver could feel himself turning cold with outrage. "Sir, your aunt was there also, and she agreed."

He was about to ask the man when he had last received a paycheck from either Ms. Renbrook or his aunt, but knew it was far more satisfying and efficient to slay the dispatcher than it was to wring the messenger's neck.

It had taken a long time to develop a sophisticated temper. He'd trained his ire to be quietly sarcastic, sharp-tongued, and toxic to humans stupid enough to tamper with him. He hadn't thrown a royal, blood-curdling fit in many, many years. However, that didn't mean he'd forgotten how.

"Holly, I'm sorry I missed your call this morning," he told her machine, his temples still gently throbbing in the aftermath of his wrath—though it was late in the afternoon. "I waited to call. I thought you might be sleeping, but I see you're up and out again . . ." he said, picking up the framed picture on his desk. The waiter he'd paid to take care of it and deliver it to his office the next day, had come through. Big tips always paid off.

The photograph could have been of anyone's hands. He liked to think they were his father's and his, but they could just as easily be his and maybe a son's someday.

"I really hate this machine. I'd much rather talk to you in person. Please call me when you get in. Oh, and use my private number. It'll ring here at the office and at home. It's . . ."

❖━━━━━❖

"Oliver? This is Holly. I'm relieved to know that your private number doesn't ring *everywhere* you go." She giggled. "I'll be home until six, then I'm off to Berkeley. Did I tell you that I go to school on Monday and Wednesday nights? I'm getting my master's . . . to impress the money people. I mean, it's not like I'll be able to do more, or be more qualified to do what I already do. It won't even get me a pay raise. I guess the theory is that the more degrees you have, the more trustworthy you are to handle grant money. I don't know. Anyway, I'm not sure when I'll be home after that, so try and call before six. I miss your voice."

"Holly, I had a dinner meeting. I didn't get home until just now. It's . . . seven-thirty. Damn." He sighed heavily. "I'll call you first thing in the morning. I'd rather talk to you tonight, but you've been out all day and I know you didn't sleep last night, so get some good sleep." A long pause. "I wish I were with you."

"H'lo."

"Hi. Wake up, sleepyhead. It's first thing in the morning already."

Oliver squinted at the clock. "Six-thirty."

"That's right. I'm on my way to work, but since my first thing in the morning and your first thing in the morning are obviously *worlds* apart, I thought I'd call you. Good morning."

"Hi." He sat up in bed and pushed the hair out of his face. "Jeezus, when do you sleep?"

"When it's convenient."

"You're going to get sick. You work too hard."

"I never get sick, and I have to work hard." There was a smile in her voice. "Say something nice so I can leave for work. I hate being late."

"Nice, huh. . . . I got tickets for Debussy yesterday. For January sixteenth. Is that good for you?"

"I'll make it good for me . . ." she lowered her voice to be blatantly sexual, ". . . I'll make it good for you too."

"Holly . . ."

"Oliver, I have to go. I'm going to be late."

"What about tonight? When do you get home from work?"

"About six-thirty."

"Dinner, then. I'll meet you for dinner."

"Oh, Oliver, I can't. Tuesdays we do condoms and needles."

"You do what?" He sat straight up. "Holly?"

"We pass out condoms and needles to the prostitutes and addicts downtown."

"On street corners?"

"That's where they are. Some of them come to us, but most of them don't. So we go to them. I have to go. Please, Oliver. Have a good day, okay?"

"Holly?"

"Yes, Oliver?"

"Be careful."

"I promise." The line went dead.

—————◆————————————◆—————

"Holly, it's ten-thirty. I was hoping you'd gotten to every drug addict and prostitute in Oakland by now. I guess not." A heavy pause. "I hate sitting here and thinking of you out there. Aren't there karate experts or sumo wrestlers to deliver stuff like that? Couldn't you drop off boxes of condoms and needles on every street corner and let them help themselves?" He sighed. "Sorry. I know better. I just don't like it. Call me."

"Oh, no. You're sleeping," he said to the muffled noise on the other end of the line. "It's six-fifteen. I thought you'd be up."

"It's what?"

"Six-fifteen."

"Oh, gawd! Oliver, I overslept. I never oversleep. I'm late. I'll call you tonight. I promise. Bye."

Enough was enough. Oliver was in love and he could hardly keep the woman of his dreams on the telephone long enough to tell her—that is, if he could get her on the phone at all.

He needed to see her. He had to touch her. A single kiss would put him into orbit. Damn her. Didn't she know?

He spent the afternoon plotting, but it was hard to figure a woman like Holly—a selfless, dedicated woman. It was just his rotten luck. An imperial command was out, she had no respect for his money or his power, and he had no authority over her—yet. Whether or not he ever would was something to consider—but maybe at a later date. No, at this point he was going to have to show his flexibility; his willingness to yield to her cause; his receptiveness to her work.

On the other hand, complacency stuck in his craw. He was not the most malleable man alive, nor was she the most judicious. She needed him to make her see reason. If she wasn't more careful, she'd work herself to death, or get hit in the head for the loose change in her purse, or fall through the floor of that run-down apartment building and break her damn neck—and miss out on the most incredible sex of this century!

Sex. She definitely needed him.

He didn't care what it took. He was going to make her make time for him. He'd collect appointments. Set up dates a month in advance. Move in with her and catch her fifteen minutes at a time if he had to. But he was going to see her.

At six-thirty he was parked in front of her apartment building waiting for her to come home from work. They needed to talk. Really talk. And phone tag wouldn't cut it. It was going to have to be face-to-face.

An hour elapsed before he took a piece of paper from the breast pocket of his suit and with his gold pen scribbled, *Must have regular, consistent work hours.*

Two hours. He wanted coffee and needed a facility, but knew she'd be home any second now. . . .

Three hours.

Four hours. It was dark. It had started to rain. It was chilly . . . and he was hotter than hell.

At eleven-fifteen he used his rearview mirror to watch

the municipal bus pull to a stop at the other end of the block. A woman stepped off and the bus pulled away. She was wearing a long, dark raincoat, passing in and out of the shadows along the street, heading in his direction. Her head was bent and her step was weary—some poor woman who had to work dawn to dusk to support her children, no doubt. She was tall and thin and—

"Where the hell is your car?" he bellowed, jumping out of his, slamming the door and stomping toward her.

"Don't come at me in anger, Oliver. I have ten brothers. I can hurt you till you cry," she said simply, unafraid, unperturbed, un-everything—except depressed and worried and tired.

He was hardly intimidated.

"You don't even own a car, do you?"

"They're bad for the environment."

"And . . ." he said, his voice still rising.

"And I can get to wherever I want to be by bus or BART."

"And . . ."

"And I can't afford one."

"I knew it. I knew it. And this is California! How can you not afford to have some sort of a car? Everybody and their mother's cousin has a car in California. Except you. No. You have to walk the streets at night and at the crack of dawn and God only knows when else, to catch buses and trains, to spend time with degenerates and prostitutes and drug addicts, and. . . . What?"

"Are you finished?" she asked, having come to a standstill in front of him. She had to tip her head back a little to look him in the eye, and she did so calmly and without flinching.

"No. Dammit. Where have you been? I've been sitting here since six-thirty. I thought that was when you got home from work."

"It's Wednesday. I had school."

"Don't you come home first? Don't you ever come home? You've been gone since six this morning."

"I went to the hospital. There was an incident last night."

"An incident?" He scanned her from head to toe. She looked to be in one piece. "What sort of an incident."

"A pimp beat up one of his girls, so I took her to the hospital. I stopped by to see her." She turned and started up the stairs to the door.

"For Chrissake, Holly, what if he'd decided to beat you up too? Don't you think of things like that?"

"If I did, I wouldn't be there."

His jaw worked erratically, but nothing came out of his mouth. With an effort he pushed out a growling noise with a tail of four words: "Hold it right there."

She released the door handle and turned to face him. He was being a pain in the butt and getting on her nerves —nerves that couldn't take much more stress.

Semicomposed, like a man talking to an idiot, he held out his hands and slowly asked, "If you know that it's dangerous to be in places like that, why do you go?"

It was a fair question, but she didn't like his attitude. She stood on the top step and leaned forward, into his face, to say, "Because *you* won't go."

"Me?"

"You. And all your snooty friends. And all the damn politicians and bankers. All those middle-class people out there who think that life at Roseanne Conner's house is as bad as it gets. Wake up, Oliver. If stupid people like me don't go, who the hell will?"

Her outburst stunned him. Good. She took a couple of deep breaths to calm herself and lowered her heavy satchel of books to the ground.

"What do you want from me, Oliver? Do you want me to get all decked out in silk and go to fancy restaurants with you? I'll do that. Do you want me to stand around at elegant cocktail parties and pretend to be brainless and beautiful? I can do that too. Or would you like me to stay home and rub your feet and cook your meals and wash your clothes? Well, I can do that, too, but not all the time. I have a life, Oliver, and I want you to be a part of it. You have a life. And I want to be a part of that. But I can't choose one over the other."

"I won't ask you to," he said, accepting the truth as he heard it. It was all of her or none at all, and that included her work. "I'm not even too sure I'd want you to. I don't like what you do. To be honest, I hate what you do. But I respect and admire it. Can't I be proud of you and worry about you at the same time?"

"Sure you can. I'm glad you are, but . . ."

"All I want is time, Holly." He took one step up to be at eye level, to show her how much he needed her. "Not a message. Not a phone call. Real time. With you. I'll take what I can get . . . but I'll get what I can take too." His mouth closed hard and fast over hers, a shattering contrast to the soft, slow sweep of his tongue. He cinched her in his arms.

Oh, to be lost in the sweet bliss that was Oliver, she thought. She pressed close, as if she were stuck to him. She was his fare, ready and willing to be eaten alive.

"Oliver," she said, her voice faint as she held him off with her hands, her forehead to his. "Oliver, wait. I need to know . . ."

"What?" His body was screaming for her, and his mind wasn't going to be much of an obstacle. She'd have to talk fast. He urged her on. "What?"

"The money, Oliver. Why'd you do it?"

"The . . . ? Oh. I . . ." Okay, a slight detour, his mind insisted. He took a deep breath and let it go. Then he shrugged. "It's money. A donation. I didn't think you'd hear about it so soon."

"But why?"

"I wanted to. Don't you need it?"

"Of course we do, but why the stipulations? Why is it for the clinic only? For management and maintenance?"

"Because you said the place was falling down." Plainly, her standards weren't all that high, so he'd imagined it as a heap of rubble already. "And I know for a fact that you don't get paid enough for what you do."

"But the building's not all that bad, and I get paid enough. The people who come there need it more."

"You don't get paid enough."

"I do," she persisted. "I make plenty of money."

"Then what do you do with it? Spend it all on your flashy cars and your swanky apartment? Holly, come on. You deserve more. So do the others."

"So, you did do it because of me," she said in an odd voice.

"Well, not *just* because of you," he said, hesitant, unsure of her direction. "But it's certainly because of you that I knew about the place and what's happening there and that it needed more money. Is that what you mean?"

Relief and happiness lifted the weight in her chest and the tightness in her abdomen. He didn't know. He really didn't know. She had suspected as much. She'd hoped. But it was good to know for sure.

"Wait a second now," he said, alarmed, setting her back an arm's distance. "You're not thinking it was a bribe or an inducement for . . ." Oh, Lord. It did look bad.

"For what, Oliver? Sex?" The dim porch light showed every nuance of his expression. It made her heart ache in the nicest way, but she couldn't help laughing. "We both know you're too smart to try to buy me."

"It isn't something I'd put past me, you know."

"But why buy what you know you can have for free?"

"When?" he asked pointedly, his hands tightening the hold on her shoulders.

She took both of his hands into hers and held them to her breast.

"Well, that depends," she said.

"On what?"

She broke loose and ran, saying, "On who gets to the bed first."

She went through the door, and he tripped over her satchel. He grabbed up the bag and followed. She was past the first landing, taking the steps two at a time, and she was laughing. It was a sound that made the old building seem bright and new again. It banished the gloom and covered the creaks in the stairs. It was a joyous noise, a titillating noise, a noise he'd have followed to the end of the universe.

SEVEN

He stumbled through the open door breathlessly, just in time to catch pillows flying and the sofa unfolding. She threw herself down in the middle of it, trench coat and all, panting and declaring, "You lose, Oliver."

Three flights of stairs weren't what they were in college, he determined, his hands on his knees as he sucked in air. And Holly was as slick and sly as an eel. This was a good thing to know about her.

"So what must I forfeit?" he asked, an all-American good sport when he wanted to be—and when sex was imminent.

"All your clothes."

He came slowly upright. His startled gaze met the bold challenge in her eyes.

"You want our first time to be like this?" he asked, just this side of stunned.

Her body was out of control with excitement.

"I want every time to be like this," she said.

Her smirk was provoking. And there was something

keenly uncomfortable in the idea of standing naked before a woman he was attracted to, who still had all her clothes on. He amended his notes on her strange perception of romance—this was beyond anything he had imagined. But then again, so was she. He deliberated a second longer, then easily decided his ego was manly and proud, and prepared for any challenge.

Deliberately, he closed, locked, and chained the door —a gesture that symbolized not safety but captivity. An allusion to demonstrate that while he was about to make himself vulnerable, she was the prisoner and in far greater peril.

She crossed her ankles and leaned back on her elbows and watched his raincoat and jacket come off. She forced herself to appear cool and collected, but her heart was pounding in her throat, her hands were tingling, and she felt a need to draw in huge amounts of air. She was battle-ready, staking her will against his. Her self-control against his determination. Her power to seduce against his need to conquer.

"Aren't you going to dim the lights and turn on music for this?" he asked, pulling his silk tie free of his collar.

She shook her head.

He slipped off his shoes and made light work of the buttons on his shirt, his gaze locked on her face. Her expression was avid but unpledged. In the silence, they could hear the building growing older as the seconds passed, and it made the friction between them grow doubly quick and strong. It was him and her, their bodies and the relentless tension, with no distractions. It wasn't long before his self-consciousness and feelings of foolishness were replaced by an empowering call to extract a reaction from her.

It was there, in the dark shadows of her eyes, in the tautness of her shoulders, in the dryness she licked from her lips and tried to swallow from her mouth. The intensity surged when he stepped to the end of the bed to remove his shirt and started on his belt buckle.

He looked down on her with eyes darker and deeper than the secrets of hell. Her skin prickled. Anticipation twisted in her abdomen. Desire pulsed between her legs. He was going to win, she feared, feeling as if she might faint dead away before he finished.

He was too strong, his confidence too overpowering. His thoughts were too plain, his ambitions toward her too clear. His shoulders were thick and broad with corded muscle, his chest wide and rippled. Sun-kissed skin lay smooth and taut over softly rounded mounds of sinew that could cradle or crush.

He shuffled out of his pants and socks at once. Her raincoat might just as well have been a sauna. She was hot. She was wet. She was weak. It was suffocating.

He stood tall, tempting, and tempestuous before her. The pressure between them mounted, like an invisible storm. Electric. Disruptive. Frightening.

She startled him when she moved, sliding to the end of the bed. He was wary of her and watchful, ready for any move she made.

"Everything, Oliver," she said, her voice thick and heavy.

"You ever think of being an auditor?" he asked. His gaze meshed with hers as he hooked the elastic of his briefs with his thumbs.

"No. But I've known my share. They don't let you get away with much, do they?" she asked with a wicked smile.

He'd come this far, he thought, sliding his shorts to his knees and working them down from there with his legs. This was her little party—he'd have his later.

She stood. She walked slowly beyond his peripheral vision. He waited for her to come around him from behind. He filled his lungs with air and waited. His nerves were stretched raw.

"You're beautiful, Oliver," she said, passing before him. Her hand reached out to glide up his inner thigh, slide past his arousal, and cruise over his lower abdomen. "I don't think there's a scratch on you."

She took another survey, her hand slipping across his ribs, coasting over his rear end, drifting across his sleek exterior as if she were thinking of buying him—or a classic Studebaker.

When next their gazes met, he almost laughed. She had what he liked to call that oh-God-take-me look he'd seen so often on a woman's face. But he didn't laugh. With Holly there was more to it. It was like oh-God-take-me-forever-and-always-I'm-trusting-you-not-to-hurt-me-I'm-believing-in-you. She really knew how to pressure a guy.

That made him smile. He was ready for her. He was ready to take on the stress and strain that he knew loving Holly would bring. He was ready to laugh and cry with her, ready to cheer her when she was down and listen to her bitch about the world when it crossed her. He wanted to hold her hand in the dark and eat the meat loaf she left cooking too long. He wanted her. All of her. And he was ready for her.

She was smiling, too, when she placed both hands flat on his chest. His heart was beating so hard, she was afraid it would bounce out and hit her in the face.

His hands turned to fists at his sides. He knew what was coming and lowered his head to make it easier for her.

She could hear his rapid breathing and feel the tension in his body. Tilting her head slightly, she outlined his lower lip with the tip of her tongue. Muscles jumped and contracted, rigid as steel bands beneath her hands. He was like the most tolerant of the ferocious jungle beasts, pushed beyond his endurance, set to pounce, awaiting the crucial, lethal moment.

Often—too often—she had a tendency to push her luck.

"I want you, Oliver," she said, kicking off her shoes.

He didn't dare move. Didn't dare breathe. Her hands left his chest to reach behind and lower the zipper of her dress. He heard the soft snap of elastic.

There was a most exquisite and wholly stirring moment of uncertainty before she spoke again.

"Is it okay to tell you that I love you?"

He gave her a stiff-necked nod.

He kept trying to warn her that he wouldn't be responsible, couldn't tolerate much more, wasn't in any shape to be toyed with, that he didn't want to rush it but . . .

She broke eye contact for a fraction of a second when she shrugged out of the top of her dress and bra, then slid everything else to the floor in one quick movement.

"It doesn't scare you? My loving you?"

He shook his head, swallowing hard as he glanced down at her nakedness. Wave after wave of excitement washed over his body, depositing layer upon layer of frustrated needs and untapped passions.

And he wasn't scared?

Well, maybe he was, just a little—of exploding. But he wasn't afraid of her love. It was almost . . .

"It's almost as if we've always been like this," he said, marveling as he looked deep into her umber eyes to see footprints, side by side, deep in the sands of time. "Always."

She worked his fists open to slip her fingers between his. She stepped closer, the tips of her breasts barely touching his chest as she pressed her lips gently, tenderly to his.

It was Christmas morning, prom night, the day the orthodontist removed the braces, Graduation Day, the driver's license in the mail, finding Carolann, the first kiss, the first paycheck, the end of a job well done . . . it was every long-awaited moment of her life and then some.

He squeezed her fingers between his. His lips played over hers, teasing and tasting. The pressure increased. His mouth grew greedy. Bare flesh met bare flesh in a glorious dance conceived during the birth of time. In a savage motion he grabbed her thighs, pulling them apart as he lifted and locked them around his waist. He turned and lowered them both to sit on the bed. He cupped her breasts in both hands. Her fingers clutched at his shoulders as her head lolled back, her back bowed, and she moaned blissfully as he feasted.

Pagan blood boiled. Hearts tattooed a rhythm of celebration, and the world retreated, leaving one man and one woman, alone, on a common quest.

'Twas the day before Christmas Eve and all through the apartment house, not a creature was stirring, not even . . . she shuddered, wondering if there was anything in the mousetraps under the sink and behind the radiator. She hadn't checked lately, but suspected it would be a good time to invite the little boy from 12C back for cookies and milk.

It was too bad the bigger rats of the world couldn't be disposed of as easily, she thought, cuddling closer to Oliver, filling her mind with his scent. Her heart ached with happiness when his arms tightened about her and, in his sleep, he shifted his weight to accommodate her.

He didn't know. She closed her eyes and offered a small prayer of gratitude. His donation coming the same day as the letter from the Carey Foundation, advising them that the grant given to the Joey Paulson Clinic was being reevaluated for renewal after the first of the year, was too much of a coincidence. It hadn't made sense that he would be giving and taking away at the same time.

He didn't know. Because, as with most large bodies of money, the Carey Foundation was run by a small horde of objective and, as in most cases, indifferent lawyers and accountants, and a handful of bored and indifferent advisers. He was simply a figurehead to the foundation, with no responsibility in it's day-to-day operations. She'd have bet her last penny that he couldn't name five organizations receiving funds from the endowment bearing his name.

And that was all right. She didn't expect him to be superhuman, didn't expect him to be any different than other rich men with vast financial responsibilities. She understood the delegation of responsibility. She understood that he couldn't be everywhere, do everything, know everything, and still speak in coherent sentences, or still be beside her in bed, his warm body wrapped around her like a protective comforter.

She understood and she didn't expect, and she was glad he didn't know that his foundation was about to put her out of work, not to mention close another door to hundreds of needy people. How could she love him otherwise?

And she wasn't going to tell him, she decided, as the sun tried to illuminate the gray skies with morning, turning darkness to dim light at the windows. He wasn't responsible for her life. She didn't need him to fight her battles or to use his influence to get her what she wanted. She'd go to the hearing and she'd state her own case. She'd make that finely dressed, well-fed committee see the need to keep the Paulson Clinic open. She was a money-people manipulator, that's what she did, and she was good at it. She was glad he didn't know.

"Those gears in your head are keeping me awake," he said, sliding down in the bed, then sliding back up, tipping his face into her neck. "What are you thinking about? It's too early to be thinking."

She laughed softly, rubbing her toes together as he kissed a path ear-to-ear along her neck.

"I was thinking it was time to get up, but I could be wrong."

"A rare find. A woman whose mind is as flexible as her body."

"A horny contortionist?"

"Those are hard to find too," he mumbled, pushing the sheets lower to expose her breasts. His hand ran smoothly between them, across her abdomen, a little farther south. "I love watching your eyes." He kissed her quickly. "They sparkle like gold dust at first, then they turn molten like liquid gold, hot and flowing."

"Yours get darker," she said, her breath gaspy, her body tensing in excitement with the play of his fingers between her legs. Her hand rose to his face. "Black. Like an abyss. I'm afraid I'll fall in."

He took her hand and lowered it to the bed, finding the other fisted beneath the pillow. He raised his body and settled it over hers.

"Go ahead and fall in, Holly," he said, separating her legs with his knees, looking deep into her eyes. "It's safe."

Would it be safe to fall deep into Oliver's soul? It called and spoke to her in a voice as familiar to her as . . . as anything she'd ever known before. There were still so many things she and Oliver hadn't talked about, so many things he hadn't yet told her, but it didn't seem to matter. She knew him. Where she might have tested any other man's worthiness, she innately believed in Oliver.

Oh, he would surely disappoint her in his humanness, she knew. He wasn't perfect. He would be angry and moody and forgetful and commit a hundred other imperfect acts, just as she would. But always his heart would be open to her. Always his soul would be faithful. And never would his mind scheme against her.

Until the day he died he would . . . Until the day he died . . . Something deep in the recesses of her mind tore loose. Even after the day he died . . . even after . . . Something free-floating and indecipherable pulled at her memory. Even after . . .

A moan of intense pleasure escaped her as he suckled her breast. Consciousness narrowed to sensation alone, to feeling without choice or control. The fragmented memory was gone. Every nip to her flesh, every touch of his tongue, was sweet torment. Her arms extended at her sides, her muscles aching with splendid expectation as he dribbled kisses across her ribs, nibbled and tasted the soft quivering skin of her abdomen. Palms parted, fingers locked in joyful battle, as he spread her legs wide and plunged her over and over again into the infinite chasm between pain and ecstasy.

Suddenly he was with her, above, beside, within her. Together they were one, a whole. Together they traveled time and space. Together they knew absolute fulfillment. Together they were life.

Wrapped in a damp towel, he left her in the bathroom to do "girl stuff." Feeling clean and refreshed after a shower would never mean what he'd thought it meant before he'd taken one with Holly. He grinned and shook his head in recollection. Nothing would ever be the same with Holly . . . or without her, he realized, falling back onto the bed, enjoying the coolness of the sheets against his overheated skin.

He wallowed in the sheer delight of being happy and within the sound of her voice for a few more minutes, then rolled over on his empty stomach.

"I'm starving," he wailed pitifully.

"Gee, Oliver," she said, coming to the bathroom door with a look of shock and disgust etched on her face. "Don't you ever quit? I can hardly walk."

When he frowned at her, she grinned—he grinned back at her proudly.

"I need food now," he said, defining his appetite.

"That's what I like about you, Oliver. You keep all your most basic needs wrapped up in the same general area, and you don't need more than a bath towel to do it."

He laughed but didn't deny it. She padded into the kitchen in her bare feet and robe, and he rolled over again like a puppy waiting to have his tummy rubbed.

"What are all these?" he asked, reading the titles on her bookshelves upside down.

"All what?" she called back.

"These foreign dictionaries?" There was a whole shelf on foreign languages alone. A few on the next shelf about customs and religious practices in different countries.

"Poverty doesn't have any trouble crossing language barriers," she said, appearing above him with two steaming mugs of coffee, one light with sugar. "Only people do. Would you like fruit or cereal? It's your lucky day. I have both."

"Cereal's fine," he said, sitting up and taking both cups from her. He set hers on the bookshelf and sipped at his own. "How many languages do you speak?"

"Only Italian and Spanish really well," she said from the kitchen. "You can't grow up in L.A. in a house full of Spoletos without speaking both of those fluently. You wouldn't believe how many times I had to volunteer to clean the bathroom at home until I caught on to enough Italian to claim some other chore." She returned to the bed with two bowls of cereal and a carton of milk. "One bathroom and all those boys." She grimaced and shuddered with disgust. He chuckled. "And then the short time I spent in the city, when I first came up here, I felt like I needed to learn Chinese. At least enough to ask the questions I wanted to ask and to know what they were saying about me when I walked away. Do you want sugar on that too?" she asked, nodding at his bowl.

"I'll get it," he said, standing. "And don't look at me like that. I'm more afraid of being shot in the head than I am of eating too much sugar."

"Did I say anything?"

"You didn't have to. So, who do you know that speaks Vietnamese?"

"There's a whole Vietnamese community here. Most of them speak English, of course, and French, and we don't see all that many of them, but we get a few. Some of the older ones bring their children with them to interpret. I'd rather speak to them directly."

"Why? What difference will it make?" he asked with no prejudice, simply curious. He came back to sit beside her on the bed, his flakes sugared indulgently.

"It's more polite for one thing, and it shows a genuine interest for another, and it's important to learn because the more you know about the language, the more you learn about the people." She took a spoonful of cereal into her mouth, chewed, and then added, "About their customs and the way they live and what they need to survive here."

She continued to eat as if they were talking about something as plain and mundane as a television commercial, not the keys to international peace. And yet, for Holly, it was just that much of a routine; that ordinary to treat everyone with polite and equal kindness, to know and understand them, to give what she could.

And who gave to Holly? he wondered, watching her eat. She didn't live much better than those she helped, and he knew it was a calculated choice on her part. There were better jobs, more money, nicer apartments. Could job satisfaction compensate for having so little to call her own?

He wanted to drench her in silk and jewels—fake furs, because she wouldn't tolerate the real thing—and cars, a dozen cars, and a big fancy home with bodyguards. He wanted to give her everything before she even knew she wanted it, anticipate her every wish, fulfill her every need. Keep her safe, shield her from all unhappiness. He sighed. Most of all, he wanted not to be angry or impatient or critical of her when she turned her nose up at it all.

"What are you looking at?" she asked, glancing up to catch his love-lights on. "I told you in the shower it was the last time. I have to go."

"Don't you ever have a day off?"

"Today is my day off."

"Then where are you going? You said work."

"I said go. Every Thursday I *go* to St. Augustine's. I do hair there."

"You do what?"

"Hair," she said, smiling. She took his empty bowl and placed it with hers on a table, then turned to her chest of drawers to gather clothes for the day. "I used to visit at St. Augustine's. Just go in and talk, you know? But it got harder and harder to sit and watch the nurses and attendants working and—" she shrugged, "—one day I picked up a brush and went to the next bed and brushed the lady's hair. Then I went next door and got the two men in that room and then two more ladies and then I hit the wards. I was crazy that day. I went from bed to bed making the men handsome and the women look beautiful . . . sort of. Then one of them said there was no sense brushing dirty hair, so I washed his hair, and one lady wanted to know if I knew how to give perms and I said that I would know how by the time I came back, and, well, things sort of snowballed after that." She laughed. She lifted her hand in a high-class fashion. "The residents make appointments now at Cheveux de Holly. They come in hours too early and sit and talk and wait for their turn."

He ran a hand over the back of his neck, trying to open his mind to the life she led, then stopped mid-motion.

"This is volunteer work, isn't it?"

"Of course. They couldn't possibly afford a real hairdresser," she said, shaking out a pair of jeans. "Although I did go to beauty school for a while, after I fried a poor old lady's hair to nearly nothing. What a mess. But I learned to give perms and simple haircuts, and I'm cheap."

"How cheap are the supplies you use?" he asked,

puzzle pieces falling from the sky and fitting perfectly. "You buy everything yourself and donate it to St. Augustine's, don't you? You pay for the permanents, the shampoos, the conditioners, the—"

"For crying out loud, Oliver. It isn't that much. We're talking about short, thin gray hair here. I can color three heads with one bottle of dye and give two perms with one kit. It's not that big a deal."

It was that big of a deal when her bed folded out in a shoebox in a run-down neighborhood! But for some reason, he couldn't make his tongue move to tell her how crazy she was to be so unselfish. It was too much Holly. It was the way she did things. It was also an answer to one of the many questions he had about the way she lived. He was going to have to be satisfied with that.

She stopped and looked across the room at Oliver. His resigned expression pulled at her heart. He was trying so hard to be an open-minded modern man and not follow his cave-man instincts. Her steps were slow as she approached him. She bent at the waist to kiss his uplifted face.

"Oliver, I love you. I have everything I need. And now I have everything I've ever wanted. There's time enough for us. I promise." She kissed him once more. "They look forward to Thursdays. I look forward to Thursdays. I'll be done by five, and if you come back here at seven, I'll have dinner and music and soft lights ready for you."

He smiled at her, and she blatantly batted her eyes at him. He laughed. Grabbing the front of her robe, he pulled her to stand between his legs, his hands sneaking inside to run up the back of her thighs to her softly rounded backside.

She caressed his face—such a wonderful face—and fingered a few strands of dark damp hair off his forehead. His hands were warm and sensuous on her buttocks. Tender and gentle and soothing. There was so much love in him, and all he wanted was the time to give it.

"You'll be exhausted by seven," he said. "I'll take you out."

Her smile turned sly. "If you pick up Chinese, we could eat it in bed."

"Hello, dear. Am I disturbing you?" his aunt asked over the phone. But before he could answer, she went on, "I've been so worried about you since yesterday. You stayed away last night, and there was no answer at the apartment downtown. . . . Are you still angry with me?"

"No." How could he be angry and in love at the same time?

"Well, my goodness, you were so upset, I didn't think you'd ever forgive me."

"You are forgiven." But the incident wasn't forgotten. "However, I prefer to sort out my own messages from here on. All right?"

"Yes, dear." She sounded pensive.

"What else can I do for you?"

"Nothing, dear. I merely wanted to remind you about dinner tomorrow night. You've been so busy, you've forgotten to call Barbara and invite her."

"Invite her to what?"

"Dinner, dear. It's Christmas Eve. You always call and invite her to have family dinner with us."

"No. You always call and remind me to invite her."

"All part of the tradition," she said, laughing gaily.

"Well, why don't you invite her this year, Elizabeth. I'm not sure I can make it."

"Not make it? But, Oliver, it's Christmas Eve. . . ."

She went on talking about family and holidays and traditions, and all he could think of was Holly. Christmas with Holly. His first Christmas with Holly—the first of many. He wanted it to be special, one they'd never forget.

"Elizabeth, I have to go," he said, braking in on the importance of celebrating with loved ones and the uncertainty of life and whether or not certain older relatives would be alive for the next holiday. "Invite whoever you like, and I'll try to come. And set an extra place, because I might bring a guest."

"But what about Barbara?"

"She can bring her own guest."

What a day. What a day. Oliver was well pleased with himself by the time he pulled into the parking lot at St. Augustine's. He'd been a very busy boy and had still managed to arrive in time to pick Holly up. He told himself it was to save her a bus ride, but in truth, the sooner to see her, the better. It was his new motto.

He hadn't been in many convalescent centers . . . well, never had been, actually, but St. Augustine's didn't look much different from a hospital. The smell was certainly the same, and the long halls with doors and the infirmary-green paint and the eerie silence that covered distant, unfamiliar noises and the overwhelming aura of pain and disease.

Hospitals were hospitals, in his book, and St. Augustine's was sure as hell a hospital, he decided, feeling immediately uncomfortable.

"May I help you?" asked a young woman in a medical uniform of white pants and a blue-and-white-striped top. She zoomed past him in the lobby, through a doorway, and out again. "Not that I can help you much," she went on as if she'd been standing still. "I'm still in orientation and I can't even find the bathrooms in this place, much less anyone to help me change the sheets in two-thirteen, but . . . I'll try. I hope you're not selling anything."

"No, I'm looking for someone," he said, smiling at the frazzled woman.

"Thank heavens. I'm pretty good at finding the patients." She pulled a sheet of paper from her pocket and opened it. "Who is it?"

"Ms. Loftin?"

"Loftin. Loftin." She ran a finger down the list. "Room 307. Take that elevator up two floors and then you're on your own. Sorry. It's not always like this, and I hope I'm not always like this, but we're short-staffed today and I'm watching the desk and the phones and helping with the residents and . . . well, as soon as flu season is over . . ." She bustled away muttering. "Flu season, my butt. I bet it's always like this around here. They're just afraid to tell me, afraid I'll quit, and I should. . . ."

Frowning and uneasy, he walked to the elevator. There were long corridors on either side where there seemed to be more activity and a little less confusion than in the lobby. Light streamed in from huge windows on both ends, dispelling some of the gloominess. There were Christmas decorations everywhere—some looked to be older than the building. An elderly man in a wheelchair waved to him and, feeling foolish, he sent a small wave back.

There was a nurses' station directly in front of the elevators on the third floor, but it was as empty as the reception desk in the lobby.

However, he was far from alone. People with walkers, wheelchairs, and canes where shuffling and limping in the halls. Some were tied into wheelchairs with harnesses and appeared to be parked in the hallway.

"Are you the magician?" He spun on his heel to see another blue-clad attendant. "You don't look like a magician."

"I'm not."

"Oh. Well then, what can we do for you?"

"I'm looking for room 307."

"It's right down the hall here, I'll show you." She turned to a man with a walker and said, "Mr. Pope? The dayroom is that way, remember? Why don't you follow this man and Mr. Stevens and me? I swear I can't tell one end of this place from the other myself today. Say, would you mind helping Mrs. Quinn there?" she asked, directing Oliver's attention to a smiling old woman in the tinsel-trimmed wheelchair beside him.

"Alls I need is a little push to get me started, dear," she said, pointing down the hall. "That way. That way. That's it. Now just give me a good shove."

Oliver looked to the attendant for help, and she

grinned at him, nodding. "She likes to feel the wind in her hair."

When in the Twilight Zone, do as the Zonies do, he thought, grimacing as he gave the wheelchair a little push. It was an incredible relief to see that he could have shot the old lady from a catapult and her wheelchair wouldn't have gone any faster than if he'd been pushing it slowly.

"Sorry, I couldn't resist that," the grinning aide said, motioning to the left with her head. "Three-oh-seven."

"Is it always like this around here?" he couldn't help asking.

"No," she said, maneuvering them around a man sitting trancelike in the middle of the floor. "But with the magician coming and Christmas and the carolers from the elementary school tonight, we're all a little excited."

"I see," he said, looking back at the man.

"You know, you look familiar. Have we met?"

She didn't look familiar, but . . . "We could have. I was at your fund-raising party last week."

"That's right. The serial killer. Are you looking for Holly?"

"Yes. I thought I'd give her a lift home."

"I'll tell her you're here, then."

"Thanks," he said, stepping out of the parade to the dayroom. "I'll wait here for her."

"Sure you don't want to come see the magician with us?"

He was positive. "Maybe next time."

Oliver was stunned. How could Holly live like this? he wondered, turning back to room 307. She worked in poverty and spent her days off in bedlam.

The woman he'd declared to be pregnant at the party passed by with another group of fun seekers. He smiled at her and received a stiff, polite nod in return. Her followers were somewhat younger than the first bunch, but all appeared to be equally infirm or impaired. Farther down the hall were some still younger.

He was out of his depth. The handwritten label on 307 said Loftin, so he stepped inside and closed his eyes.

Was it the reminder of his own frailties that was turning his stomach? Or was it worse? Was his sense of human perfection insulted by the sight of physical disease and weakness? He was trembling inwardly and castigating himself for his own weaknesses, those of his mind and his heart. It was one thing to believe in the dignity of the human soul, and quite another to act on those beliefs. It would be bigotry of the first order if he couldn't find some way to connect the belief with his actions.

It grew quiet in the hallway. He sighed and slowly opened his eyes. He felt sick at the pit of his stomach. Every resident he'd seen was a supreme being, compared to the low he was feeling. And Holly . . . What would she think of him? Lord, how he wished he was more like her: so open, her love all-encompassing and so easily given.

He looked about the room then, confused. Not an office. Not a storeroom of hair supplies. A dim light glowed across the room; the overhead was off but a fan rotated slowly from above. A bed with a brightly colored patchwork quilt. An old wooden chest of drawers. A small artificial Christmas tree. An easy chair and another lamp. He stepped to the center of the room.

There in the shadows sat a woman . . . or a man

with long hair, dark but mostly gray. No, a woman. She was looking straight at him.

"Excuse me," he said, mortified. Had she been watching him all along? Why was she so quiet and still? Was she afraid of him? "I beg your pardon. I didn't mean to disturb you. I have the wrong room."

He shifted into reverse and was making a hasty retreat when his eye caught the marker above the bed. Loftin, Carolann. Carolann Loftin? Loftin wasn't all that uncommon a name, but it wasn't that common either. The years he spent worshipping his Uncle Max weren't a complete waste, he knew, as he calculated the odds of a particular hospital accommodating two women by the name of Loftin, one a patient, one a volunteer. He stepped closer.

"Are you . . . You aren't by any chance related to Holly, are you?" he asked.

She remained silent and motionless.

"Holly Loftin? She works here? Does hair? She's a volunteer?"

She remained silent and motionless.

He moved closer, bent at the waist to get a better look. Maybe he was mistaken. Maybe she was asleep. No. She was staring at him—straight through him, as a matter of fact. He inched forward.

She sat in the wheelchair with her hands settled one atop the other in her lap. She wore a canvas vest over shocking red pajamas, tied to the back of the wheelchair to keep her upright.

She remained silent and motionless.

"My name's Oliver Carey," he said, not sure why, coming to a crouch position beside the wheelchair. He searched her stonelike features for similarities, and even taking into consideration the ravages of time, pain, and disease, he found none. The woman had never been a beauty, but then Holly wasn't what some people would categorize as a classic knockout. Holly had a good face, a nice face, an animated face, but her beauty came from within. Her beauty was in her . . .

He reached out and slowly turned the lamplight to the woman. Her eyes were golden brown, a rich umber, an earthy color. Watery, they shimmered like tarnished gold dust. They were Holly's eyes, but without the warmth and the wisdom.

He pivoted toward the sound of movement at the door.

"I see you've met my mother," Holly said.

EIGHT

"So what do you think, Carolann?" she asked, crossing the room. "Didn't I tell you he was handsome?"

Oliver stood as she approached them, watching her, baffled. As if she'd done it a thousand times under the same conditions, she stretched up to kiss his numb lips.

"Hi," she said, smiling her pleasure at seeing him.

"Hi." His voice squeaked.

"He's tall too," she said, back to addressing Carolann as if it were a three-way conversation. "I like my men tall, don't you? Comes in handy when you have a lot of stuff on the top shelf, doesn't it?" She smoothed her hand over the coarse hair she'd brushed and secured at the neck with a pretty new clip first thing that morning, and smiled at Oliver. "What have you two been talking about?"

"I just got here," he said, dumbfounded. He had a hundred questions to ask, but by the way she was acting, it didn't feel like the right time or place.

"Have you been properly introduced?"

"Yes. I told her who I was." He felt like an over-achiever taking full honors for a simple task poorly done.

"Good. She keeps to herself mostly, but that doesn't mean she isn't listening. Right, Carolann?" She bent to be at eye level. "I'm leaving now, but I'll be back tomorrow. It'll be Christmas Eve. I'll sing to you. We'll open our presents on Christmas morning again this year, if that's okay with you?" Holly kissed her mother's limp cheek, hugged her, and patted her shoulder. "Bye. Sleep well tonight," she whispered.

She stood and chuckled at Oliver's expression. "Say good-bye, Oliver," she reminded him.

"Good-bye Oliver" was on his tongue and halfway out his mouth before he could stop it. Everything felt so unreal. It was either make jokes or scream hysterically.

"Good-bye. It was nice to meet you, Mrs. Loftin."

Holly laughed. "Ms. Loftin, if you please. Carolann never married."

He was getting curiouser and curiouser. He could barely contain himself while Holly gathered up her coat and the bag she always carried, said good-bye once more, and moved out of Carolann's room.

"Oh, where to start," she said, flinging her arms through the muddle of new things to talk about before he had a chance to say a word.

"Try the beginning," he said, not at all surprised that she was ready for his questions. If she'd been in his head again recently, she wouldn't have seen anything but a huge question mark.

"Hmmm . . ." She was thinking. "I guess it started when the Spoletos tried to adopt me. I was nine. I was in school and I wanted to receive my First Holy Communion. I went to Catholic schools, did I tell you that?"

"No."

"Well, I did. But I started late. I didn't know anything about the religion, so I was nine before I could get baptized and receive Communion the way Mama and the boys had. I wanted to be like everyone else I knew. I always felt so left out of everything. But there are rules against indoctrinating foster children into a religion without the court's or the natural parents' permission.

"Mama knew how important it was for me to fit in and feel normal. She didn't like making waves with the Child Welfare people because she was always afraid they'd take me away if she did, but she thought it might be worth it this time. She thought God was something I'd be able to take with me wherever I went. But the judge turned her down flat. So then she decided she'd try to adopt me. I'd already been with them a year and a half, maybe two, and there hadn't been any parental contact, so she tried.

"Good night, Linda. Good night, Rosa. I'll see you tomorrow?" she said, as they passed two attendants in the hall. "Then have a nice holiday. I'll see you Monday.

"Where was I?" she asked, her fingers finding his hand and slipping in comfortably.

"The Spoletos were trying to adopt you."

"Oh, yeah. Well, after talking to me and the people from social services, and with Mama's other adoptees, the judge thought that might be okay, but there was still one hitch. My birth mother was alive and she hadn't relinquished custody." She paused briefly, glancing down at the floor. "This was news to me. Hurtful news. I'd always thought she was dead. I didn't know her. I didn't know anything but foster homes."

"Holly, I'm sorry. You don't have to tell me any of this."

"Yes I do," she said, stepping into the elevator. "You need to know. You need to make a decision as to whether or not you can live with who I am."

"It doesn't matter, Holly." He could see the hope in her eyes, and that she wasn't quite ready to believe him on this point. He wanted to shake her. He wanted to do something, anything, to convince her that nothing in her past mattered to him—maybe it was one of those things that only time could prove, he thought. "All right. Go on."

They left the elevator, crossed the now-posted lobby, calling farewell to a nurse as they went. They stepped out into the cool, fresh evening air. Oliver couldn't remember smelling anything better—except maybe Holly, warm and musky with passion.

"Well, she wasn't dead and she didn't want me, but she wouldn't give up custody either. So, there I was. And when all my friends were going up to receive Communion, I was sitting in the pews. And when they all marched up to get confirmed, I was sitting in the pews. Mama did her best. She'd tell me it wasn't as important to receive the sacraments as it was to be prepared, in my heart and in my soul, to receive them. It wasn't much of a consolation. And every time I'd be left sitting in the pews, I'd think about her, my real mother, the one I'd thought was dead."

He helped her into his car, and she waited for him to slide in beside her.

"It didn't end there though. Do you have any idea how much paperwork is involved with a foster child? Every time something happens? Getting a driver's license and applying for state loans for college were like getting an amendment added to the Constitution. Mama and I would sit there and roll our eyes and fill out papers till our fingers went numb." She laughed, looking out the front window at nothing in particular. "Carolann Loftin gave me life, but Marie Spoleto made it worth living. She's a tough old cookie. Nothing was too big for us to handle together."

"So, how did you find Carolann?" he asked, after a short silence.

"Why. I should tell you why I found her first. And I'll tell you I was angry," she said, the emotion clear in her voice. "I hated her. I hated her with all my heart. I hated her for every time someone laughed at me or called me a name or called me Spoleto and made me explain. I hated her for giving me away, and I hated her for not giving me to Mama. I hated her every time the social worker came to our house, and Mama would worry that the house wasn't clean enough, or that I was too thin and would they take me away from her. I hated her for making me different. I hated her when I was afraid and lonely. I hated Carolann every time I looked in the mirror." She went silent.

Oliver was glad. He didn't want to hear any more. He was curious, but it wasn't worth listening to Holly relive it in her mind.

When she spoke again, it was on a lighter level.

"So when I graduated from college—now, you have to remember that I studied psychology and sociology and

I was young and innocent and a terribly deep thinker at the time. . . . So I had decided that in order for me to purge myself of all my unhealthy and pent-up anger, I would need to confront my birth mother and tell her exactly what I thought of her," she said, like a college professor.

"And you put her in a coma?"

He was as shocked by his words as she was. They looked at each other across the car. Then suddenly burst out laughing.

"Oh, Oliver. That's awful."

"It's sick. I can't believe I said it. I'm sorry," he said, shaking his head, his gaze darting back to the road.

"Don't be," she said, still chuckling. "It's better to laugh sometimes."

He was hesitant to hear more, leery of his own responses, afraid he might add to her pain. But she was right. He needed to know—he wanted to know all there was to know about her. Not to pass judgment, but simply to know.

"What did happen? How did you find her?"

"I was twenty-two by then, so I petitioned for full disclosure of my files. I got her name and her last known address from there." She paused. "Chinatown. San Francisco."

"Chinatown?"

"That was her last *known* address. There were about twenty more after that. It took me almost eighteen months to find her," she said, getting out of the car at the curb in front of her apartment.

"She was here in Oakland," he concluded, coming around the car to join her.

"No," she said, speaking carefully. "Her records were here, but she was in a mental institution."

"Napa State?"

She shook her head slowly.

"Vacaville," she said, as if the word alone were enough to make her tongue bleed.

"Holly," he said, repulsed as much by her discovery as by the ordeal she must have gone through to make it.

She opened the outer door and walked in.

"She didn't belong there. She hadn't hurt anyone, she was just . . . sick. It was the first available bed, some-place to dump her. I couldn't bear seeing her there, so I spent the next four years with doctors and lawyers and judges, trying to get her out. What a terrible place," she muttered, taking the stairs. "It took every penny I could scrape together and more time in courtrooms than I'd spent in classrooms all through college, but I finally got her out. About three years ago. St. Augustine's isn't the Ritz, but it's clean and they treat her well . . . and we can afford it."

"We?"

"Me and the State of California. We struck a deal—I leave them alone forever, and they pay half her expenses, which are as much as they'd be paying for a state facility anyway, only now they have another bed for some other poor soul that no one knows what to do with."

She knew she was being awfully hard on the practice of psychiatry, a field of medicine few understood and fewer still could tolerate. She knew it was an area of limited choices for the doctors, the families, the victims. She knew her option to take Carolann out of the institution wasn't available or advisable for everyone. She knew . . . but it didn't change the way she felt.

"Do the Spoletos know about all this?"

She nodded as she slipped the key in the lock.

"I finally had to tell Mama," she said, walking in, kicking off her shoes, and shedding her coat all at once. "When I got sick—remember I told you about when I died that time? I couldn't pay my hospital bill. I'd listed her as my next of kin where I was working, so the hospital went to her for the money.

"She paid it, of course, but then she came for a visit," she said, rolling her eyes heavenward. "I'd been flying back and forth and telling her everything was fine and wonderful and I was making all this money and . . . well, she came to see for herself." She motioned about the room with her arm and then slid down onto the couch. "You wouldn't believe the fit she had when she saw this dump."

Oliver's brows rose. So, it wasn't a deep-seated political statement against the system. She didn't live in a hole-in-the-wall by choice! He wanted to fall on his knees and give worship. There was hope yet for a bigger bedroom and a mattress without lumps.

". . . and you know she never travels alone," she was saying. "Bobby and Tony came too. Two more fits. The neighbors thought the Mafia was invading and wouldn't open their doors for days. Lord, what a mess it was, and I was still sick." She shook her head. "I didn't stand a chance."

"They do give you money, then? They help out with Carolann?"

"They did for a while, until I got her settled and

found a job I could keep. I kept getting fired for taking too many personal days and skipping out to see lawyers," she mentioned as an aside. "I wasn't an ideal employee. But later, when I could manage, I asked them to stop."

"Why?"

"The Spoletos are kind, loving, and generous people. They're also very proud people. They make it on their own. They don't live off one another; they make their own lives. And I'm as much Spoleto as I am Loftin. I can manage on my own."

Another puzzle piece found its niche. He thought it ironic that along with an overdose of the Spoleto pride, she'd also picked up more than her share of the generosity and was absorbed in giving away every nickel she earned.

"Were they hurt when you told them what you'd been doing for Carolann?" He sat down beside her.

"I think the boys were, a little, maybe. Maybe they felt they hadn't been enough to make me happy or they'd somehow let me down in some way that made me go looking for her. But Mama understood. Right from the beginning, she knew why I couldn't hate her anymore."

"Why?"

She shrugged. It all seemed so simple now, so obvious. "She gave me life," she said. "And she didn't have to. It was the late sixties, of course, and abortion wasn't legal, but that doesn't mean it wasn't readily available. Especially to people like her."

"How do you know what she was like?"

"I read her files. The first thing I had to do in all this was declare myself her sole relative and get custody of her. Then I could get into her files and talk to her doctors and hire lawyers." She shuddered. Her aversion to doctors and lawyers was nearly as great as it was to money people. "She was a . . . a runaway—from some dinky town in Idaho. A hippie, I guess. A nothing. Someone who fell through the cracks.

"There were a bunch of drug arrests before I was born. And by the time my birthday rolled around, we were both heroin addicts. That was in my file too. I was premature and sick for a long time—I was lucky they could find so many foster families to take me," she said thoughtfully. "I suppose that also accounts for all the not-so-nice people I met in Chinatown when I first came up here, and for the obsessive-compulsive tendencies in my personality."

His chuckle was a snort of agreement. She smiled too. She couldn't deny that working too hard could be as harmful to your health as shooting drugs, but she did prefer to think of it as a more productive means to the same end. She was still working on that flaw.

"There for a time, though . . ." she started, then seemed to get buried in the thought.

"What?" He shifted his weight to extend his arm across the back of the couch, his fingers immediately tangling in her shiny dark hair.

"There for a time, she was in and out of clinics, hospitals, rehab units as if she were trying to get clean? Like maybe she was trying to get straight so she could be with me? I don't know. Maybe it's what I want to think. Maybe I want to believe that she okayed the private schools because it was good for me and nixed the religion and the adoption because she wanted me back. Maybe I've been fooling myself, I don't know." She sighed. "I'll never know. By the time I was seventeen she was psychotic from the drugs. A paranoid schizophrenic averaging nine months a year for the next four or five years on psych wards and in mental institutions. She was catatonic for two years before I found her."

"So, she doesn't talk? Ever?"

"Nope. She's pretty quiet most of the time. She gets excited once in a while, and you have to sort of scrape her off the ceiling, but . . . not too often. And the people at St. Augustine's are pretty cool about keeping her. I mean, it's not as if she'll ever get any better. And that is pretty much the general idea behind the word 'convalescence.' "

"Those people are going to get well?" he asked, trying to imagine it, thinking of miracles.

"They're all trying. They all want to. Some will even go home for short periods. None of them are considered permanent residents—except Carolann. You weren't comfortable there, were you?"

"No," he said, feeling coldhearted.

"It's okay, you know. To feel human. It's scary to see yourself in those people. The trick is to look at them with your heart and not with your mind. I used to do that with Carolann all the time. I look at her and wonder . . ."

"What?"

"How she got that way. Not the drugs, but . . . Why? Why her and not me? Why some people's lives just run down like clocks till they stop. Why some people get tossed away like old tennis shoes. Didn't anybody tell her what was happening? Couldn't anybody see what was happening to her? Didn't anybody love her the way I was loved?"

Oliver lapsed into silence, trying to digest all that he'd heard—the story, the emotions in Holly's voice, Carolann's plight. He didn't know what to say. Something in him wanted to apologize, but how could one man ask pardon for the whole world? He would have given anything to make it all different for Holly, for Carolann too.

"So? What do you think?" she asked, sitting up and turning to face him. "Can you still love someone who sees fried eggs with a side order of bacon and thinks of her mother?"

The gentle smile in his eyes told her first, but then he closed them, cursing life. Why should she have to ask? Why would she wonder? Why didn't she simply know, take it for granted, assume it, take it as a fact as solid and unchangeable as needing air and water to survive?

When he looked at her again, his gaze was direct and unwavering, twinkling with humor, dark with the determination to settle the issue for all time.

"If that someone is you, I can still love her," he said, stroking her cheek with the back of his fingers before he turned his hand over and curved it around her neck. "I could love you if you had a horn growing out of your forehead," he said, kissing her there. "I could love you if had one big eye here, instead of two beautiful eyes, here and here. I could love you if you had a nose like an elephant or lips like a platypus." Her giggling made kissing them difficult, so he pulled away to look at her. "There's only one thing I could never tolerate."

"What's that?" she asked, glancing down at his fingers as they began to swiftly work the buttons down the front of her shirt.

He stopped to tip her chin upward, to make her look at the truth in his eyes.

"I could never tolerate not loving you," he said, clear, plain, and simple.

And maybe because it was so clear, plain, and simple, she believed him. She didn't ask herself why or what it was about her that he loved. She didn't question his sureness. She didn't speculate on a time span or examine the difference between them. That they loved each other was a truth written in stone by the firm hand of Fate, fixed, preserved, unalterable.

He kissed her with confidence, slowly, firmly, deeply. With a possessiveness originating long before they shared a plane ride to L.A., long before he yearned to find his soul mate, long before the creation of man.

He peeled the woolen shirt from her shoulders and grabbed at the cotton T-shirt beneath it, and when he couldn't get close enough to her, when he couldn't spread her body out beneath him, to toy, to tease, to tantalize, he muttered an oath and stood up.

The shock of cool air on her heated skin and the sudden tilting of her careening senses as he grabbed her hips and pulled her flat onto the couch, opened her eyes. It amused her to watch him fighting with the cuffs of his shirt in his eagerness to put flesh to flesh.

"What's your hurry?" she asked, grinning.

"No hurry," he said absently, flicking his belt buckle open and pulling her hips lower in the time it took to blink.

She waited for him to lower himself over her, to see his eyelids grow heavy with satisfaction, to feel his heart pounding against her breast, to wallow in the rapacious expression of his face when he had settled his body comfortably, perfectly atop hers.

"I know what you're doing," she said shrewdly.

He grinned. "Good. I'm a little too far gone to take the time to explain it."

"No, I meant that I know what you're *really* doing."

He tilted his head to one side and scanned her face. "Okay. What am I really doing?"

"You're trying to distract me."

"That's right. I am," he said, lowering his face to the curve of her neck. Her body trembled as he tasted her. It shuddered as he kissed her and took tiny nipping bites of her soft, sensitive skin.

"It isn't going to work," she said, her voice hardly convincing.

He looked at her with a smirk on his face, his eyes asking, "Wanna bet?"

"It isn't," she insisted, unaware that she was grinning back at him when she sternly continued. "I know what you've done, and this isn't going to work."

That took care of the smirk and had him frowning.

"You forgot to bring dinner, didn't you?" she said. "And now you're hungry and thinking that if you give me a little lovin' I'll forgive you and jump up afterward to make you something to eat."

"Oh, yeah," he said, tipping his head from side to side. "It just so happens, Ms. Smartypants, that when I'm responsible for the meal, we have it my way, and I prefer dessert *before* the main course. However, in this particular instance, dessert *is* the main course."

"Huh?"

"You said dinner at seven and we'll eat at seven. It's
. . . six-fifteen now, so lie back, shut up, and enjoy this."

"Wow, you're bossy," she said, laughing, squirming
with delight as he plopped fat wet kisses across her chest
until his mouth covered her breast.

He suckled till he heard the low moan in her throat
and felt the arc in her spine, then his head turned to enjoy
the other, and he muttered, "You're a pain in the ass."

Dinner was served promptly at seven . . . on delicate china, from silver serving trays, by tuxedo-clad waiters from Won Chow's, a very elegant Cantonese
restaurant in San Francisco. Candles were lit and four
dozen roses were set about the room in cut crystal vases.
Sterling silver utensils were laid out on fine linen—but
Holly was accomplished at chopsticks and had more fun
feeding herself, and then Oliver, as they lay wrapped in
sheets, happy and replete on her lumpy bed.

"Here, you read yours first," she said, handing him a
fortune cookie.

He shimmied up in bed, broke it open, and read,
"You will get lucky again tonight."

"Oh, stop. That's not what it says. Give me that."

"No, no. You're right. It says, 'If last name rhymes
with "Jerry," you will get lucky again tonight.' "

"Oliver. Let me see that."

"No, no. This is my fortune, and I like it. Read your
own."

She popped half the cookie in her mouth and chewed
as she unfolded the tiny piece of paper, scooting down in

bed beside him. She clucked at him in disgust and then laughed.

"How did you do this?"

"Read it."

" 'If first name rhymes with "trolley," you'll get lucky too.' "

NINE

"Are you sure this dress is all right?" she asked again, turning herself in the mirror, frowning over the color.

"It's perfect," he said, trying not to sound surprised. Other than the floral print dress she'd been wearing when they first met, he hadn't seen her in anything but jeans. The red dress she wore was a definitive statement in simple elegance—and a relief, as it was one less thing for her to be troubled about since he'd invited her to his home for Christmas Eve dinner. "You're perfect. Stop worrying."

She let him turn her from the mirror and allowed one heartening kiss, but her mind was beset with misgivings. The dress being the least of them.

Oliver was unaware of the workings of the Carey Foundation, but his aunt, Elizabeth Carey George, was not. This she'd discovered long ago after many phone calls and meetings with the finance managers. The committees held their collective breath for a thumbs-up or -down from Elizabeth George, for without her support and fund-raising endeavors their hands would be tied with short purse strings.

Then, too, there was the cold reception she'd received from Elizabeth when the family had come to Spoleto's at Thanksgiving. She didn't really care what his family thought of her; they didn't have to like her or welcome her into Oliver's life with open arms . . . but it would be nice.

And finally, there was Oliver. He was calling the affair a family dinner, not because it was family only, she gathered, but because it was a smaller do than was usually launched at his house, and because only the family and fifty or sixty of their closest friends were invited—no strangers. No matter what he thought of her, or how highly he regarded her, she would be a stranger tonight —a poor, unconnected, socially uncelebrated stranger from Oakland.

Oliver knew who and what she was. He knew where he was taking her. He knew the risks. She sensed enough of the old arrogant, rebellious Oliver to know that if she didn't make a good impression on his friends and family, he'd turn his back on them before he turned it to her—at least at first. But there was still a chance that his ties to his world were much thicker than the material money was made of. He could come to resent the fact that she couldn't fit into his world as easily as he'd slipped into hers . . . maybe not consciously, but certainly subconsciously, and then what?

It was a test they had to put to their love sooner or later. A test that shouldn't matter, but did. A test she could pass with ease if it weren't for people like Elizabeth

George and Barbara Renbrook, who also, it so happened, held the fate of the Paulson Clinic in their hands.

"Take a deep breath and relax," he said, handing her out of the car in front of the house. It looked like the Library of Congress. "You're as stiff as a mannequin. If I'm crazy about you, they'll be crazy about you. And I'm very crazy about you."

"Oh, Oliver. You're not really thinking that way, are you? You're in for a big disappointment if you think all these people—"

"These people are a lot easier to please than I am, believe me. I didn't think there was a woman worth loving until I met you. Trust me. You'll have them eating out of the palm of your hand in an hour. Even my aunt will come around, once she gets to know how much you have in common with her. Cause is her middle name, and Lord knows you have your share of them."

"Her middle name is Carey, Oliver," she said, thinking old, proud money and blue bloodlines.

"Holly, my name is Carey, and I love you."

He did. And it was important to remember that. If she walked in the huge double doors cringing, she'd never pull it off.

"Okay," she said, stopping beside some tall shrubs she thought would conceal her. She shook her hands and drew in a deep breath and then another. She straightened her spine and affixed a bright smile to her lips. "Okay. I'm ready."

He laughed aloud. In less than ten minutes she was going to feel like an idiot, and he was looking forward to it.

If the outside of the Carey mansion looked like a

library with huge tasteful wreaths hung on the doors to celebrate the season, the inside was even more overwhelming. The space was inspiring, like a church or a cathedral. The decor artful and understated. Sinfully, she kept wondering how many homeless families could take shelter in an area that size—and then realized that they hadn't yet left the foyer. She got a little dizzy with her calculations.

"Ah, Clavin," she said under her breath when the man appeared. He wasn't at all what she'd expected, a tall, thin man with a natural air of authority, pressed and tidy, but very unstuffed and unstarched. It was his broad smile and cordial "Good evening and Merry Christmas, sir" for Oliver and his warm welcoming eyes and friendly "How do you do, miss" that tossed her over the edge of nervousness and into a place where anything was preferable to screaming and pulling her hair out.

"Tell me, Clavin," she said, humor twinkling in her eyes as she handed him her wrap. "Do you belong to some sort of butlers' union? Is there an organized force to ensure your labor rights? You shouldn't take any chances, you know. With unemployment the way it is and the cost of medical care the way it is . . ."

"Oh no you don't," Oliver said, laughing after his initial shock. He should have expected her to warm up to Clavin right away; everyone did. He had hoped her uncharacteristic display of nervous jitters would last at least until he got her to the living room. He was rather liking the idea of being her only ally in an enemy camp. "I didn't bring you here to start an insurrection. Keep her away from the gardeners, Clavin," he said over his shoulder, pulling the two apart. "And tell Cookie that if she didn't make those little round nut cookies that I like for Christmas this year, I'll have her flogged."

"Yes, Mister Oliver."

"Mister Oliver? Is that what he calls you? Mister Oliver?"

"Now that I'm the one who pays him, it is. When I was young, he called me 'young hellion' or 'brat,' and once he spanked me with a wooden spoon."

"He did?" She was impressed. "What for?"

"Stealing his *Playboy* magazines."

She gasped in shock and then had to gasp in shock again as they walked into the crowded living room and came face-to-face with Phil Rosenthal.

"Holly! How wonderful to see you again so soon," he said, coming to take her hands in his and planting a fond kiss on her cheek. "I thought I'd have to wait a whole year. Marge, come see who's here."

Oliver stepped back, smiling. With Marge Rosenthal came Bill and Jane Gastrel, who introduced Holly to the Burkes, who were delighted to introduce her to the Hallerons, who laughed at her humorous remarks on the last Rams and 49ers game and introduced her to the Dorseys. She was passed around like a plate of delicious hors d'oeuvres, and his friends were gobbling her up.

He liked seeing her in his house. Things he hadn't really noticed in years took on new meaning. He wanted to show her everything. He wanted her to be comfortable there, to grow fond of a piece of furniture or a couple of the paintings or to a particular room. He wanted her to become attached to something, to anything he owned, and then, maybe, someday she might be able to call the place home.

"There you are, dear," his aunt said, coming up behind him. "You're late. I was so hoping you'd be here to help greet our guests. . . . Oh, hello," she said when she saw Holly, an expression of surprise and vague recognition on her face.

"You remember Holly, don't you, Elizabeth? I introduced you in L.A.?"

"Yes. Oh, yes," she said, also recalling the name from the incident with the telephone messages as well. "I do recall."

Holly smiled and extended her hand. "It's nice to see you again, Mrs. George, and Merry Christmas. Thank you for inviting me tonight."

"Yes, certainly, dear, you're welcome, but to be perfectly honest, you're my nephew's surprise guest this evening. We had no idea who he was bringing," she said, as if, had they known, they might have canceled the party.

"Oh. Well, I hope I won't be an inconvenience."

"Certainly not, dear," Elizabeth said after a quick glance at Oliver's intense expression. "There's plenty of room for one more," and then, thinking to cover her disappointment with humor, she added, "and please don't feel you need to clear away the dishes. We have plenty of help tonight."

Those in the crowd who knew Holly went silent because they didn't understand what Elizabeth meant. The others went silent in confusion as well, but because it was a strange thing to say to a guest, period.

Elizabeth looked around, knowing immediately that something had gone wrong. And as all eyes were on her, and because Oliver's were particularly unnerving, she felt she needed to explain her little witticism.

"She's a waitress, you see, and I didn't want her to feel it was necessary for her to . . ."

"Oh, Mother, really," Johanna Reins said, stepping out of the silent crowd to save Holly. "She's not a waitress all the time. She was helping out her family that night, remember?" She turned to the gathering. "If none of you have been to Spoleto's in L.A., you'll have to make a special trip. It's fabulous. I heard about it from Jacqueline Spears—and you know she knows her restaurants." Everyone laughed. "Holly's family owns it, and you really must go. We went at Thanksgiving, and I'm still trying to lose the weight I put on that night."

Johanna slipped an accepting arm about Holly's waist and, turning her back to both her mother and Oliver, walked into the crowd with her new best friend.

"Oliver, dear, I didn't mean . . ."

Oliver turned to his aunt, and she fell instantly silent. He looked at her hard and long, seeing only a pathetic, bitter old woman. In a soft voice that carried both a warning and a threat, he said, "Remember where you are, Aunt."

"But I didn't mean . . ." she faltered. He had walked away from her. And the only other person under her own roof who seemed even the slightest bit interested in hearing her explanation was dear, sweet Barbara Renbrook. Always willing to listen, always willing to understand.

"You're not going to start humbugging, now are you?" Holly asked Oliver a short time later. She'd caught him alone and brooding by the fire. The fireplace was big enough to comfortably sleep four, she noted, bringing her total to 784 people so far.

"Of course not," he said, turning to her, smiling.

"Now that I've got you where I want you—on my turf—I don't have anything to humbug about. I just wish . . . I'm sorry about before. I wanted everything to be perfect tonight. I wanted you to see how normal people with money can be."

She smiled. His choice of words amused her.

"Well, I appreciate the thought, but 'normal' connotes a standard, and this"—she waved her hand to include the house as well as the party gathered—"isn't standard anywhere but on one extreme end of the economic pole. *However*, I do like your choice of friends. They're nice people."

"For rich people."

She grinned. "For any kind of people."

"Did you really think I'd fill my house with people like my aunt and then bring you here as a sacrificial lamb? You were pretty nervous earlier."

"No . . . Well, yes, but not intentionally. I forgot about the Rosenthals and the Gastrels. I knew you wouldn't let anyone hurt me, but I also didn't want you to have to defend who I am to your friends."

His expression drooped. "You mean, instead of watching you flirt with every man in the room, I could have been slaying dragons? I blew my chance to impress you with my studliness?"

"I don't flirt," she said, batting her golden eyes at him. Then, grinning wickedly and stepping closer, she added, "And I'm already impressed with your studliness."

He felt chills all over his body.

"There's a bed upstairs," he said, bending his head to her ear, "that's big enough to sleep eight." Her eyes grew round, not because of the size of the bed, but because he was using her yardstick to describe it. "We could go up and roll around on it for a while."

"What about dinner?"

"We could roll around in that too . . . and then we can spend the rest of the night cleaning each other. The tub's big enough for four. Plenty of room for two."

"What about your guests?"

"They'll have to use the other tubs."

"Should I ask how many tubs there are? Or just let it go?"

He laughed at her disdain.

"Since I'd have to tell you that I don't know exactly how many there are, maybe we should change the subject," he said wisely. "Have you met Senator Berryman yet? Big money. Excellent contributor. Good target for St. Augustine's. Oh! And the Weirs. Very deep pockets . . ."

Holly spent the rest of the evening biting her cheeks as Oliver passed her from one guest to the next, irreverently slipping her bits of information and amusing anecdotes under his breath. Side by side, they were a charming, handsome couple, and everyone noticed how deeply in love they were—apparently.

"Everyone's talking about it," Johanna insisted, meeting Holly in the powder room after dinner. "They've never seen Oliver so happy or so obviously in love. It's very plain that you're good for him. He's actually having fun tonight."

"He doesn't have much fun, does he?" she said, thinking of the sadness she sometimes saw in his eyes, the loneliness.

She had reapplied her lipstick and run her fingers through her hair and was now leaning against the vanity, content to stay and talk with Johanna, whom she was liking more and more.

"Not much anymore. Not since he took over for his father and then started acting like him too."

"You make settling down sound terrible."

"No," she said, thoughtfully reblushing her pale cheeks to perfection. "Not terrible. But in Oliver's case, it's definitely boring. I really miss the old Oliver sometimes."

"I understand he was pretty wild."

"Wild." She grinned in the mirror at her. "Good word for it. He was a wild man for certain. And fun, except when he felt like fighting. He was constantly getting into fights. We used to go out and do wonderfully crazy things together. We were forever in trouble." She paused and became wistful. "He's full of guilt and responsibility now, but underneath it all, deep down inside, there's still a wild man. He still gets crazy now and then." She looked up at Holly. "Like the other day when he exploded all over my mother for dismissing your phone calls."

Ah. Now they were on a subject Holly really wanted to get into. She'd discover all there was to know about Oliver in her own way, in her own time, and enjoy every minute of it. But she didn't have that luxury with Elizabeth George. She needed information and an operational strategy for her right away.

"Oliver and your mother fought about me?" Not good news.

"Oh, I wouldn't call it a fight really," she said, putting

her makeup back into her beaded purse. "It was more like Oliver clouding up and storming on her, and her standing there getting wet. You see, my mother's . . . uh . . . a little narrow-minded, but she isn't stupid. Everything we have belongs to Oliver. He's very generous, and don't get me wrong, he doesn't hold it over our heads or anything like that, but my mother's always afraid he might. She's terrified of him." She turned to Holly in earnest then. "Which is one of the reasons I've been waiting to get you alone tonight. I wanted to warn you about my mother . . . and Oliver."

"Warn me about what?"

Johanna was hesitant, not knowing the right words to express what was on her mind.

"I don't want you to misunderstand me," she said slowly. "I love my mother. She's not an all-bad person. She's . . . old-fashioned. She still believes that money is built into the DNA molecule. You're either born with it or you're not. Even new money is something of a genetic defect to her. And then, of course, to keep the gene pure and undiluted, she frowns on intereconomic relationships. Money should marry money and make more money." She held up her hand. "I'm not saying I agree with her thinking. It's just the way she is . . . and she knows all about you."

Holly's eyes narrowed defensively and her body automatically shifted to a prepared stance.

"Exactly what does she know about me?"

"That you're Joan Ellerbey's right-hand person at the Paulson Clinic, and about your mother at St. Augustine's."

Holly went quiet and wary, unsure of the issue. Was it

that she wasn't good enough for Oliver? Or was it something else? Was Elizabeth planning to use Carolann as a wedge between them? Or was it something else? Was Elizabeth planning to cut the grants to both places because of her? Or was it something else?

"She's really not a bad person," Johanna persisted. "She's completely dedicated to helping those less fortunate than us. Truly she is. But . . . well, she isn't always the wisest person."

"Meaning?"

"Meaning, I think you should tell Oliver that my mother's planning to revoke the grant funds to the Paulson Clinic this quarter and have St. Augustine's reviewed next fall."

"Because of me?"

Johanna sighed and looked thoroughly shamefaced. She couldn't look Holly in the eye as she gave a slight nod of her head.

"I'm afraid so," she said, her voice shaky with regret. "I'm sorry, Holly. But that's why I think you should tell Oliver. She won't listen to me. I've tried over and over to explain to her that cutting off the funds to the clinic because of you would be hurting so many more people, so many people who need so much . . . and how good you are for Oliver. But she's not listening. Her mind is set, old-fashioned and misguided as it is. Tell Oliver. She's afraid of him, so she'll do whatever he says. She keeps pretending she hasn't made the connection between you and the clinic yet, but that's only to keep Oliver from getting suspicious and stepping into her territory. I really think he should know."

"Why don't you tell him?" she asked. It was a logical

question, if Johanna was as concerned as she appeared to be.

But she became even more embarrassed and degraded as she admitted, "I would but . . . I know how cowardly this is going to sound but . . . we live in a trickle-down budget here. My mother gets her money from Oliver, and I get mine from her. . . ." Her words faded on a pathetic note. "Please don't think too harshly of me. I . . . I'm not like you, Holly. You're brave and strong and capable. And I'm . . . I've been trained to be a rich man's wife, a party hostess, a fund-raiser, a pretty ornament. I don't know anything else. I can't tell him and risk losing everything I know. I'm sorry."

It was a disgusting confession, but heartfelt, and Holly couldn't bring herself to condemn her. Johanna wasn't like her mother. She'd been nothing but kind to Holly since their first meeting. She was as much a victim of circumstance as the people who came to the clinic—though the comparison was rather broad.

"I appreciate you telling me this," she said. The small smile of acceptance and pardon on her lips couldn't quite make it to her eyes. "At least I'll be prepared now. But I've already decided not to tell Oliver. I thought about it when we first got the notice, when I discovered he didn't have a working, hands-on knowledge of that end of his business. But I don't need Oliver to fight my battles for me, and I can't ask him for money. This is business, and it shouldn't have anything to do with what he and I have together."

"But doesn't my mother's attitude change all that? I mean, if she's going to play dirty, shouldn't you?"

"No," she said, her head lifting higher in the air.

"There's a board of trustees. We have a legitimate need for the money. There are ways of getting around this sort of thing."

"Oh, Holly, I hope you're right about this. My mother has a lot of influence over the foundation. It's her only source of power, and she guards it carefully."

She was genuinely concerned, and Holly found it endearing. She was beginning to believe she'd found a true friend in Johanna, and who knew? With a little nudge here and a little prodding there and a few more serious talks and some exposure . . . maybe Johanna would eventually make a good recruit.

"Yes, but now I have a friend on the inside, right?" she said, smiling as she put an arm around Johanna's shoulder. "Someone to keep me informed. Someone to whisper sweet nothings in her mother's ear."

Johanna grinned, slyly.

"My mama warned me about girls like you, Holly Loftin. And I'm beginning to think she's not all wrong about some things." They laughed. "But I'll do what I can. I warn you, it may not be much. I'm not a big part of the scheme of things around here, but I will try."

"Well, you're a big part of my scheme. And I need all the help I can get."

Oliver parked behind the Paulson Clinic in the alley between Deaver Street and the old library that now housed an army surplus outlet. He waited almost twenty minutes before he released a long-suffering but good-natured sigh, removed his pure-silk tie and suit jacket, then entered the two-story building through the rear entrance.

Warm, moist air, thick with the mixed aroma of the four major food groups and coated with the overwhelming scent of roast turkey, met him before he even had the door open. So did the clamor of pots and pans and the rumbling of a couple hundred voices from within.

At five o'clock that morning, Holly had slipped from the cozy warm nest they'd made on her couch to help prepare Christmas dinner for the line of people that now extended along the entire front of the building and down half the next block.

Once again she'd underestimated her generosity in thinking she'd be finished and ready to go out for their own Christmas celebration by seven-thirty that evening. And he'd accounted for that, arriving at eight. But it was now nearly eight-thirty . . . and he knew Holly.

With the uncanny ability that came with love, he spotted her almost immediately in the crowd. Standing at the serving line, talking and smiling and laughing as she worked. He took a minute to watch her, to realize that service was not only her job, but her joy. He felt his heart swell with something that was more than love; something that hurt, it felt so good; something he'd never known before.

Holly was the woman he'd waited for all his life. Strong, independent, and giving, from the top of her head to her sexy little toes. If she wondered how Carolann came to be Carolann, he couldn't help wondering how Holly came to be. Where did her bottomless well of love come from? Her wisdom? Her caring? Her humility and pride?

A person was either born with those things or not. Granted, the Spoletos had guided her well, but Holly was born with the capacity. And why? Why Holly and not him? Or Elizabeth? Or Barbara? Or Johanna? Why was Holly's capacity to love and give so great?

He smiled. It was a question it might take a lifetime to figure out, if then, and he was looking forward to investigating all the possibilities. She was a puzzle. A frustrating, irritating, intriguing puzzle. She was as predictable and unpredictable as . . . as life. His life. She was his life.

He snuck past a huge caldron of mashed potatoes and stepped around vats of peas and green salad and red Jell-O. He ducked around women with big bowls of rolls and men with carving knives, and finally settled his hands on her hips from behind.

She didn't even flinch. If someone in that neighborhood had grabbed him from behind, he'd have . . . well, he wasn't Holly, was he? She merely turned her head, grinned at him, served another helping of stuffing, and faced him.

"Hi," she said, kissing him the way she did every time they met. It was always a pleasure, but it was always amazing to him the way her quick little kiss was a sign of her happiness to see him, her acceptance of him, her ownership of him. "You're late."

"I knew you wouldn't be finished by seven-thirty."

She shook a finger at him, laughing. "Don't try to outthink me, Oliver. I was done at seven-thirty because I wanted to spend the evening with you. I know how much our time together means to you, and I was looking forward to it. But you weren't here at seven-thirty, so I got back in line. And now . . ." She looked over her shoulder at the stream of people. When she looked back at Oliver, he was wearing a torpid expression and watching her unblinkingly. "What?"

"Do I look stupid?"

"Right now? Or in general?"

He laughed at her then. It was either that or wring her neck . . . or make love to her under the buffet tables.

"Oh, stop giving me that big innocent look and move over," he said, elbowing his way to a tub of gravy. "I've got your number, babe, and you're not fooling me for a second. This was your plan all along. You're thinking that just because I know that when this is all over, you're going to be hyped to the gills with excess energy and wanting to make love all night, that I'll stand here and pour gravy on everything that passes by." He picked up the ladle and dribbled the brown liquid over an outstretched tray. He smiled at the woman holding the tray and told her she was welcome to it, then turned back to Holly. "See. You're not so smart."

"Neither are you," she said, grinning as she took up her spot over the sage dressing. "I was ready to go home and have sex on the floor an hour ago." Simultaneously they noticed the man across the table avidly listening to their conversation. "The things we have to do to get volunteers around here," she said to him, then laughed as she looked up at Oliver's expression.

"Geez, Holly," he muttered under his breath. "That guy's going to be back here first thing in the morning, offering you every service you can think of."

"Yeah, well, the things we have to do to get volunteers around here . . ."

Her dismissive giggling did nothing to ease the disapproving frown on his face. She had to lean over and murmur, "I love you, Oliver," in his ear before people started asking for gravy again.

The days were lazy and pensive after Christmas as people wound down from one holiday and geared up for the next.

"How did you manage that?" Oliver asked, following her into her apartment. "Tonight *and* tomorrow off, as if you had a regular job? What'll we do?" He paused and looked anxious. "This is our test, you know. This'll make us or break us, spending more than four hours together at one time. Gawd!" he exclaimed putting his hands to his head. "What'll we talk about? What'll we do?"

"What's your point here, Oliver?" she asked, fighting the smile that wanted to take over her droll expression.

He grinned. It had become his custom to take her into his arms whenever the opportunity presented itself. He did so now, slowly and with calculation.

"My point," he said, bending his head to nuzzle her neck, "is that I'm overwhelmed with all the time we'll have to do this to each other." His body quickened as he reached up under her sweater to feel her soft, warm skin against his palms and he heard the familiar hum of satisfaction in her throat. "If we start now, we might be finished in time for you to go to work on Sunday." He kissed her until her knees buckled, and he smiled. ". . . or not. We'll see."

She stopped the descent of his face toward hers with one finger to his lips.

"I worked Christmas so that families can be together, but mostly because New Year's Eve is my night to celebrate."

"We'll celebrate like crazy, right here on your lumpy couch."

"Nope. I want horns and confetti and champagne."

"I'll call Clavin and have him bring some over."

"I want people. Happy people."

"We'll roll over at midnight and watch Dick Clark in Times Square. He's a really happy guy."

"Oliver," she said, her tone cajoling, her smile the slyest thing he'd ever seen. "I have a new dress. I borrowed it just for tonight, just for you, to wear with the beautiful pearls you gave me for Christmas. Pretty dresses are a shame to waste, don't you think?"

He had reservations at The Mark for eight-thirty and a night of festivities planned, but it was fun to watch her in operation. Of course, he'd have canceled all of it for a chance to spend the entire time sequestered in her apartment making mad, passionate love, but he was just as willing to take her out and show her off to the town.

"A definite waste. Is it red? I like you in red. And black," he added, remembering her Freudian slip.

"You'll like me in white too," she said, pressing her body to his in all the right places. "And all night long you can think about taking it off."

He set her away from him.

"We'll see about that," he said, his voice strained, his body coiled and tense like a spring about to be sprung. "You better hurry."

She chuckled, knowing exactly how he felt and loving the notion that she could make him feel that way any time she wanted to. It was very heady stuff, love. It made her feel as if she might live forever; as if she had power over the universe and that every wish she made would come true.

"I still haven't figured out where your friends got the idea that you're such a tough guy, Oliver," she said, moving off toward the bathroom. "I think you're . . ."

"A pushover?" he said, his body aching.

"I was thinking . . . sweet," she called out.

"Don't push it, Holly." He threw his coat over hers on the back of a chair and started looking around for something to do while he waited for her to shower and change.

"Putting those little battery-operated fans on Mrs. Quinn's wheelchair, so she could feel wind in her hair, was pretty sweet, Oliver."

He cringed. It had been a simple, mindless, impulsive act on his part, and he was beginning to think he'd never hear the end of it.

"They were lying around the boardroom, from when I used to smoke," he said with a shrug, uncomfortable with gratitude and praise. "The board would sit in there with those little fans and blow the smoke back in my face."

"So you quit."

"I quit for me. I still smoke at least two cigarettes during every board meeting as a matter of principle." Holly laughed and said something, but he didn't hear. He was distracted by her answering machine. "Do you know you have thirteen messages on this thing? Don't you ever listen to your messages?"

"Thirteen?" she asked, coming to the bathroom door in her bra and panties. "I wonder who . . . Did you call earlier?"

"Yesterday. I forgot it was Thursday."

"Then I must have forgotten to erase it," she said, frowning. "I wonder who the twelfth one is?" She went back into the bathroom.

"Well, aren't you going to listen and find out?" he asked, his finger itching to press the button.

"I'll listen to them later."

"What if they're important?" He couldn't help himself, he pressed the blinking red button—it was reflex.

Holly came back to the door when she heard the machine beeping. Smiling, she leaned against the doorjamb to listen, her eyes wise and knowing as she watched Oliver's face.

"Holly, it's John. I'm just calling to wish you a happy birthday. The kids and Annie send their love, and you know you've got mine. Call when you get a minute and . . . have a blast, babe."

"Holly? It's Mama. I love you. You hava nice birthday and you call me in the morning, yes?"

"Little girl, it's Tony. Are you out with your friend Oliver again? When are you going to bring him back to meet us properly? I promise to be good and not ask too many questions. I'll even stuff a loaf of bread in Roberto's mouth. Did I wish you Happy Birthday yet? I think I forgot, but you have a good time tonight and you bring him home, you hear?"

"Holly? This is Bobby. Who is this fellow, this Oliver, Antonio talks about? I think I should meet him, yes? Just because you're having another birthday doesn't mean you can forget about your family. You call me tomorrow."

"This is me again, Bobby. Happy Birthday, little girl. I love you."

"Hol-ly! Happy Birthday! Remember when you turned twenty-one and we all took you out New Year's Eve and you said it was like having the whole world celebrate your birthday? Every New Year's I think of that and cheer your birthday more than I do the new year. Oh, in case you can't tell one message from the next, this is Tom. Bye. I love ya."

In all, there were twelve birthday messages. One from her mother, two from her brother Bobby, and one each from her nine other brothers—and Oliver's missive from the day before made thirteen.

"Why didn't you tell me it was your birthday?" he asked, disappointed that she hadn't, flabbergasted by the outpouring of love he felt from her family. His father had always remembered his birthday, but it was usually a quiet, simple thing that came and went each year without much ado. "I should have known from your name it was sometime around Christmas."

"Yeah," she said, laughing. "I used to wonder about that. Then I decided Carolann must have been strung out on something and thought it was still Christmas—otherwise, she might have named me Time or Eve or Passing or something else very hippielike. I lucked out, huh?"

He smiled. "I still wish I'd known."

"I'm glad you didn't. As you heard, I've always had more than enough to put up with on my birthday."

"But I want to get you something . . . a gift."

Wholly unconscious of her attire, she walked into his embrace and kissed him as if he were the beginning and end of all she knew.

"You *are* the best present you could ever give me."

TEN

Merchants ruthlessly removed all signs of Christmas and the New Year from their windows and within days were pushing hearts and flowers and shiny boxes of chocolates. A few moved straight into spring—setting shamrocks and leprechauns and daffodils and baby ducks in the same window.

Holly stood at one such window and wished she could make time travel as fast. She wished it were April and that whatever was to happen between that moment and then, was over and done.

The grant hearing was scheduled for the twelfth of January, eight days away, and if she were facing anyone but Elizabeth George, she might have been able to sleep soundly at night. As it was, she slept fitfully, waking often to ponder the future of the clinic, of the people it served. She made mental lists of other available grants, private and federal. She rehashed her own budget, cutting already dull corners, squeezing out every penny she could spare.

She wasn't going to give up. Between Joan Ellerbey and herself, they would find a way to keep the clinic open . . . she hoped and prayed. But then there was St. Augustine's.

Every day she went to visit Carolann and every day she wondered if, when St. Augustine's was threatened with a loss of funds, would she go to Oliver for help? She had no real influence there; she wasn't aware of the complete financial situation. Could they withstand the loss of a single grant? Or would it break them, force them to close their doors? And if she did turn to Oliver, would it be fair to do so to ensure her mother's safety, when she wouldn't do it for the hundreds of needy people at the clinic?

Holly was a gut-reaction sort of person. She acted on instinct, thrived on impulse. But lately her judgment was clouded with the dust from the battle between her love for Oliver and her pride.

He'd have given her the moon and the stars, too, if she asked. It would make him happy if she asked. All she had to do was ask, but she couldn't. She went over every reason and found fault with each. Oliver knew she didn't need him to fight her battles; he knew she wasn't after his money; he would know that she wasn't asking for herself but for countless others . . . and still she couldn't bring herself to ask.

"Will you please pay attention," Oliver spoke sternly, scattering her thoughts. "I'm not doing this for my health. I'm doing it for yours. Pay attention."

He stood before her in gray fleece sweats—formal wear at Bill's Health-o-Rama, where, for her birthday, he'd given her a lifetime membership. He'd said it was the closest thing he could find to a real gym within walking distance of her apartment and that if he couldn't make her see reason, he would at least see to it that she could defend herself.

For the first half-hour he'd coached her through a series of muscle-building exercises. He'd been wholly indelicate in pointing out what he called flab on her body, and he'd pushed her aching muscles to a point where she could have taken said flab and beat him about the head and shoulders with it.

Now he was showing her self-defense techniques—and he was a brutal instructor.

"You have to be focused. Tune into everything around you. Nine tenths of the battle is surprising your attacker with your awareness. Make it a habit." He stopped, his body relaxed, then he cocked his head to one side and asked, "Are you okay? You seem sort of out of it today."

"I'm fine. I'm tired and I want to go home and I don't think this is really necessary, but I'm fine."

"Okay," he said, taking on an attacker's attitude, ignoring her complaints. "Now, be ready and be focused. Remember, there are five prime targets. Their sight"— he pointed to his eyes—"their breathing"—nose and diaphragm—"their ability to walk or chase after you"—legs and feet—"and where they live."

She followed the direction of his hands and smiled.

"Does Clavin press your sweatpants like that, or do you wear a new pair every time you go to a gym?"

He screwed up his face at her. "At least mine are in one piece and there aren't great gaping holes to show everyone the color of my underwear."

She pulled at the elastic and peeked into her pants.

"I thought you liked these pink ones," she said, trying hard to look hurt.

"I do," he said, quickly glancing at the bodybuilders. "Everyone does. They're distracting as hell."

She grinned at him—the time-tested grin, the grin she knew made his blood boil.

"Are you going to pay attention or not?" he asked harshly, feeling a little overexerted.

"I really can take care of myself, Oliver."

"Humor me."

She sighed and rolled her eyes, ever indulgent.

"Okay," he said. "Turn around and let's say I come at you from behind. Like this. I grab you around the neck like so and twist your arm back like this. What are you going to do?"

"Scream?"

He tightened the hold on her neck enough to make her realize that screaming wouldn't help.

"Poke you in the eyes with my other hand?"

She tried, but he shifted his weight, pulled on her twisted arm, and kept her defenseless.

"Not so smart now, are you, Holly?" he said, close to her ear. "This is why I want you to learn self-defense. You're an easy target. If I wanted your money, I'd take it. If I wanted your body, I could take that too. If I wanted to bash your head in, I'd do it now. . . ."

She knew his intentions were good, but there was just something about his attitude that was starting to tick her off.

Before he could take another breath or say another word, she stomped down on his instep, and as his head reared back in pain, she twisted and rammed her elbow into his diaphragm. When he bent forward, she nailed two more targets with an upper cut, catching his nose in a hit directly between the eyes. He reeled backward on his heels, and she tapped his groin with only enough force to let him know that had she wanted to, she could have cracked his family jewels wide open.

He landed on the mat on his backside, and when he felt blood trickling through his nose he went flat on his back. When the stars began to fade and he could breathe again, he opened his eyes.

Holly stood above him, looking concerned until he opened his eyes and glared at her. Then she smiled, shrugged easily, and said, "Ten brothers."

"Your brothers taught you that?" He struggled to a sitting position, trying not to notice the delighted smirks on the faces of their bemuscled audience.

"They taught me the important stuff, but I picked up the fine points at the YWCA when I first came to Oakland and had to move into a potentially tough neighborhood." She leaned forward and helped him to his feet, looking closely at his nose. "It was great therapy while I was going to court for Carolann. I'd pretend all my attackers were lawyers. We'd better get some ice on that. Are you all right?"

"I'm fine," he said, the terse remark an indicator that his ego was bruised worse than his nose. They started for the locker rooms. "I can't believe you did that."

"Well, I didn't want to hurt you, but I figured that if I didn't, you'd never believe I could do it."

"You could have warned me."

"Surprise is nine tenths of the battle, remember?"

He gave her a sidelong glance as he wiped blood from his nose with the back of his hand.

"Are you mad?" she asked.

"No."

"Yes, you are mad. I can tell."

"I'm not mad," he said, getting angry. They stopped at the entrance to the men's locker rooms. "I'm . . . disappointed, is all."

"Disappointed? Why?"

"Well, you don't want my money. You don't need me to teach you anything. I can't do anything for you. You won't let me help. I feel . . . useless."

"Useless?" she said, laughing softly as she reached up and gently wiped blood from his upper lip. "Oliver, I'm depending on you to give me what I need the most. I need you to love me. I need you to teach me how to slow down and enjoy my life. I need your help to get through the day. I want to be with you more than anything I've ever wanted before."

He took her hand and watched his thumb rub back and forth over her knuckles.

"It's not enough, Holly," he said slowly. "It's as if you have two separate lives. The one with me and the one you struggle with day after day. I need to be a part of that too. You don't talk about the problems you live with every day, so how can I fix any of them? Make it easier for you? Make a difference in your life? I feel left out. I want to be involved in your whole life, not just a part of it."

"You want to work at the clinic?" she asked, floored.

"No, of course not. But I want more than to come over and make love to you every night, or take you out to eat once in a while. It's not enough. I want more."

She didn't know what to say to that.

Did he really want to hear how she had to beg for food or that they were running out of warm clothes in children's sizes or that the shelters were full and they had waiting lists for jobs and housing and nonemergency medical care? What would he do? Go out and buy food and clothing? Hire doctors and nurses? Invent jobs? Build housing?

And what about his aunt? What if she told him she was threatening to cut the funds to the clinic? Would he take over the foundation and would he expect Holly to tell him which charities to support and which not to? Even she didn't want that kind of responsibility.

And she didn't want Oliver thinking he had to single-handedly cure the world's ills, just to make her happy. It wasn't all up to Oliver. It was everyone's responsibility.

"Hello, Oliver?" she said, calling impulsively with her great idea. "How's your nose?"

"Swollen and I have two black eyes. Clavin sends his cheers." She covered the mouthpiece so he couldn't hear her giggles. "Are you calling to gloat?"

"Who, me? Gloat?"

"Are you laughing?"

"No way. I'm dead serious. I have a favor to ask."

"What is it?" His attitude changed instantly.

"Were you serious when you said you wanted to do something to help?"

"You know I was—I am."

"Well, I've been thinking . . ."

"There's news."

". . . there's not a lot I could ask you to do at the clinic. I mean, you've donated money and—"

"What's the favor?"

"Well, if I work at my end and you do the work that's appropriate for you at your end, would that make you feel a little less left out? I mean, it doesn't have to be day-to-day nitty-gritty stuff, it just needs to be helpful, right?"

"What is it?"

"Well," she said, finding it hard to ask, knowing it was a stupid way to feel. "There's a bill in the state senate to appropriate more funds for prenatal care, immunizations, and special ed services. I was wondering if . . . well, if . . ."

"If I could throw some Carey weight around and get it passed?" he asked with enthusiasm.

"I thought that since you sort of hobnob with those kinds of people that maybe—"

"Holly, you don't need to explain. It's a great idea, and I want to help. I'll do whatever I can." There was a brief silence. "Was it really that hard for you to ask me for such a small favor?"

"I'm not used to asking people to do what I couldn't or wouldn't do myself. But in this case, nothing I did would make any difference. You said you wanted to make a difference."

"I do," he said, and after another brief pause he added, "And Holly? Thanks for letting me try."

That Thursday she dyed three gray heads the same striking blue, gave four tight perms and ten haircuts. She listened to the hospital gossip involving two night-shift attendants and caught up on the story about Mr. Jared's niece and the Arab prince she was dating. She tried not to give any weight to the whispers about old Ed McGreevy chasing after Darleen Gibbs, a young seventy-six, but then she didn't deny any of the rumors she heard that Oliver had a serious crush on Mrs. Quinn . . . he'd sent her a box of batteries for the fans.

She told Carolann all about her problems with the Carey Foundation. She was wishing for some empathy when she began to tell her about the situation between her and Oliver and Elizabeth Carey George. She wanted advice, but got none.

It was a gray, yucky day, but dry and far from dark when she decided to walk the ten blocks home rather than take the bus. Oliver had a dinner meeting and wouldn't be coming till late, if he came at all. She took her time, walking and thinking.

One of the best things about her life was Marie Spoleto.

She owed Carolann her life, but she was never sure of her motivations. Had she given birth out of love? Or because she knew she wasn't going to survive, and that small part of her that wanted to, needed Holly to carry on for her? Or had she been so completely out of it that she simply hadn't cared one way or another?

Now Marie Spoleto, she was something else. No secrets there. Marie lived hard, worked hard, loved hard. She moved from place to place to place in straight lines. Openly, honestly, and independently. After so many years, Holly didn't need to ask her advice. She could hear in her heart the words she'd heard so many times before.

"You follow the rules, you do what you can, you say what you must, and you live with what happens."

By the time she got home she was almost done second-guessing herself. Should she? Shouldn't she? What if? What about? Her head was throbbing with questions for which she only had one answer.

"I'll follow the rules, I'll do what I can, I'll say what I must, and I'll live with whatever happens."

There was a knock on her door shortly after six and, not expecting to see Oliver until much, much later, she called out, "Who is it?"

"It's Johanna, Holly. May I come in? Please."

If she hadn't heard it in her voice, she would have certainly seen the fear in Johanna's face when she opened the door. She scooted into the apartment as if she were being chased. Holly stepped into the hall, scouting in both directions. It was empty.

"Are you all right?" she asked, noting the flutter of her hands over her heart.

"Yes, of course," she replied breathlessly, her voice high-pitched but unwavering, her eyes darting to the door as if to tell Holly to hurry and close it. "I'm fine. How are you?"

"Well, I'm great," she said, chuckling as she observed Johanna's version of Oliver's reaction to the neighborhood. "It's wonderful to see you, but I hope you're not going to tell me you were in the neighborhood and decided to drop by. I wouldn't believe you."

"No, no, I came here on purpose," she said, her hands twitching nervously at her hair and her perfect sandalwood-colored wool suit as she watched Holly close and bolt the door. "I . . . I was going to call, but I thought it might be better if I came in person."

"Would you like something to drink?"

"No, no. I came to tell you something. I . . ."

Johanna's agitation wasn't all because of the neighborhood, Holly could see now. She must have been pretty upset to drive herself to Oakland in the first place, she realized.

"Let's sit, shall we?" she said, motioning to the chair and sofa a few feet away. "It's always easier to talk sitting down."

Johanna took a couple of steps forward and then shook her head, refusing to sit.

"I can't. I . . ." She released the long strap of her purse from her shoulder and stood clutching the bag with both hands. "I overheard my mother talking to Babs—ah —Barbara . . . Barbara Renbrook this morning. They're plotting—" she hesitated, "well, this goes back a while, it's been their plan all along. I'm not sure it ever would have worked, but it might have, eventually. Who knows? But now with you . . ."

"Are you sure you wouldn't like to sit down," Holly broke in. "You're making me really nervous."

Johanna took an emotional step down and tried to smile.

"I'm sorry," she said, lowering herself into the chair. "I know my mother is capable of many things, but I never dreamed she could be so . . . so cruel."

"What has she done?"

"Nothing yet. It's the plot—the plan she and Barbara have been working on all this time. For years. You see, my mother and Barbara have a sort of friendship. They like each other and they have a lot in common—including a meeting of minds in regard to social standing?" She looked askance to detect if Holly caught her meaning, and Holly nodded. "As you can probably guess, Oliver is the catch of the century. I was always a little surprised that my mother didn't try to marry me off to him, since we're only related by marriage. But it didn't work out that way. Thank goodness," she added with a nervous giggle.

"My mother always thought Barbara would make him a better wife, and she throws the two of them together every chance she gets. Only Oliver's too cagey to get caught in her trap. He hardly notices Barbara. Oh, he cooperates with my mother to keep the peace and invites her to family functions and escorts her here and there, but he always finds other women to get involved with. And my mother lets him, thinking he'll eventually come to his senses and marry Barbara anyway. Then he met you."

Holly's brows rose with interest. It wasn't as though the plan were out of this world—she herself was planning to marry and live happily ever after with Oliver someday. It was the pain in the pit of her stomach that had her concerned and curious.

"Oliver is so plainly in love with you, you've got them shaking in their boots," Johanna went on. "Especially my mother, who is so used to handling everything at the house and getting around Oliver without another woman's interference. You're a real threat to her."

Holly nodded. She could understand that too. She wished Johanna would get to the bottom line.

"They were in the sunroom this afternoon having

tea. I was going to join them, but just as I was about to, I overheard them talking about you. So I listened." She looked to Holly for absolution, as if eavesdropping were a major crime.

"I knew you'd make a great spy," she said, smiling.

"Well, I thought you'd want to hear what they were saying about you."

"I can imagine that," she said. "I'm more interested in their plan to get rid of me."

Johanna nodded, glad she didn't have to repeat a great deal of what she'd overheard and glad that Holly had caught on so quickly.

"It's a simple plan, according to mother. She says that all she has to do is refuse to renew the grant for the Paulson Clinic and let it filter down through the proper channels that it was Oliver's decision to withdraw. And you have a reputation for fighting for what you want, so she has determined that you'll fight with Oliver, he won't understand what your talking about and get angry back, or if he does figure it out, he'll assume you were after the foundation money all along, and your relationship will be over. But"—she held up a single finger—"just to ensure it, she'll cancel the grant to St. Augustine's as well."

Holly sighed loudly and fell back against the couch, lacing her fingers together across her aching abdomen. Her first reactions were not those of fear or anger, but those of repugnance and sadness that any two human beings of her own gender could be so totally pathetic and hateful. It was a shame to call them women.

"What are you thinking?" Johanna asked, her voice small and tentative.

Holly smiled. "I'm thinking how glad I am that you're my friend."

"You're going to tell Oliver now, right?"

"Nope," she said, sitting up again. "I don't think it'll be necessary at all now."

"Why? What are you going to do?"

"I'm going to your mother. I'll tell her that if she does revoke the grants, I won't get mad, I'll get even. I'll turn the tables on her. I'm not above a little blackmail, now and again. I'll tell her that I'll tell Oliver the whole story." Her smile grew brighter. "In fact, since we still have a few days before the hearing, I'll insist I get her guarantee to reissue the grants, in writing, by tomorrow afternoon, or I'll go straight to Oliver before the hearing. That way she won't be able to come up with another plan."

"Uh-oh," groaned Johanna, slumping down in her chair in a very un-Johanna-like manner. "I knew I should have kept my mouth shut."

"Oh, that's right," Holly said immediately. "We don't want any of this coming down on you from your mother. Gee, let's see, we'll have to revise the counter-attack a bit, so she won't know it was you who told me."

She was already deep in thought by the time Johanna spoke again.

"It's too late for me. That's not what I meant about keeping my mouth shut."

"What's too late for you?"

"My mother knows we're friends, you and I. I knew she wouldn't like it, but I've disappointed her so often as it is—with my failed marriage, my lack of social leader-ship, my inability to organize even the simplest gala affair," she said with a wave of her hand. "I figured one more heart-crushing failure on my part couldn't possibly make that much of a difference to our relationship."

"She knows because of the way you've always been so nice to me?"

"Oh no, I had to tell her plainly. It's another flaw," she said, dejected. "I'm nice to most everyone. I failed Snubbing 101."

"That's a shame, but I can't say I'm sorry," Holly said, trying to make light of her friend's supposed inadequacies.

"You will be in a minute," she said. "I waited for Barbara to leave and then I confronted my mother with what I'd overheard."

"Uh-oh."

"She said that if I wanted to befriend a . . . a . . ." She stood, suddenly agitated again.

"It's all right, Johanna, say it."

". . . a guttersnipe, that it was fine by her. In fact, she was glad of it because now she could send me to you with a message."

"A message?"

She nodded. "She said she hated the idea of having so many needy people going hungry and cold on her conscience, and that she was willing to advise you on an alternate course that would change the fate of the Paulson Clinic."

"Go on," she said calmly, already convinced that she didn't want to hear the alternative, and just as sure she wanted it out in the open.

"She . . . she said that she preferred to let your conscience deal with the poor, hungry children. She said to tell you that she was perfectly willing to renew the grants to both the clinic and the convalescent center and increase them by fifteen percent each year if you . . ." Her chin fell to her chest. She couldn't go on. Couldn't bring herself to repeat her mother's vicious words.

"If I what, Johanna? Tell me."

Johanna lifted her eyes to Holly's. There were tears in them. Her chin quivered, and she chewed her lower lip for a second before she could speak.

"Walk away from Oliver."

ELEVEN

"Oh, man, you're a sight for sore eyes," Oliver said, stepping into the apartment, scooping her into his arms at the same time.

"Sore eyes is right," she said, tipping her head back to look at the red crescent moons casing the inner aspect of both his eyes, the right slightly darker than the left. "Oh, Oliver, I'm sorry. Do they hurt a lot?"

"Only when I'm not holding you," he said, squeezing her tight. She looped her arms about his neck and squeezed back, harder, until she was afraid she might choke him.

It was a little before ten, and he smelled of pipe smoke—an odd observation, but that she could make any observations at all was admirable. She felt numb through and through.

"I didn't think Larry Clark would ever stop talking so I could leave and come back here to you," he went on, his face buried in the curve of her neck. He pulled away smiling, enjoying the sight of her. "He's never been a favorite of mine, but I know now why he's on the state appropriations committee. He talks incessantly, until whoever's asking for money forgets what they came for and . . . Hey. What's this?" He pulled her into the circle of dim lamplight as he scanned her face more intently. "Are you all right? Have you been crying? What's happened?"

"Nothing. I'm fine. Really," she said. By his careful visual inspection of her body parts and expression, she could tell he didn't believe her, so she added, "I'm a little tired." He wasn't buying that either. "And Tony called," she said, as if, yes, there was something wrong. "Mama's sick."

It was the first good excuse for puffy red eyes that came to mind, other than the truth, and she didn't know what to do about that yet.

To Oliver's mind came the recollection of the last call from his father's doctor.

"Ah, geez," he said, turning to snatch up her coat, admonishing himself as he went. "See there. To hell with conservative economic reforms. This is insane. I knew I shouldn't have given up the company jet. Well, that's still okay, we can charter one if there isn't a flight out right away—"

"Oliver! No!" she said, shaking her hand free of his as he tried to pulled her through the doorway. "No. It's okay. It's not serious. There's plenty of time. She's not dying."

"Oh."

"It's just some bug she can't shake. Maybe the flu. She's been in bed for a couple of days though."

"Oh," he said, sort of coming back to earth, going

limp and looking foolish all at once. He gave a soft half-laugh and closed the door. "Well. You've been crying and I thought . . ."

"I know. I'm sorry I upset you." She didn't want him to be upset. She didn't want him to care. She didn't want him to love her. She didn't want to love him . . . but she did. She turned the clock back three minutes, stepped back into his embrace, and lifted her face to his. "Pucker up and I'll make it up to you."

Where he might have meant it to be an affectionate, pleasurable kiss at first, she changed it to something else, holding on when he might have let go, deepening the kiss when he might have ended it. And he was easily swayed. He tightened his arms about her, plunging deep and hot into her passion, stoking his own.

Holly's heart cried out to him. No matter what happened, no matter what she did or what she said, no matter what anyone else said, no matter what, he had to know that she would always, always love him.

She ripped at his coat, and he went for her blouse. His jacket and tie were next in her hands, and in his, her breasts fit nicely. Buttons snapped and breath grew warm and erratic. She was possessed by a selfish devil and wanted his soul. He loved her. She tortured his body with ecstasy, cutting her passion into his mind, destroying it for anyone else. He continued to love her. She drew him within her, captured his seed, and tore that which was Oliver away, hiding him deep in her heart, leaving only the shell. And he still loved her.

"Remind me to inquire after your family more often, will you?" he said sometime later. They'd turned the couch into a bed and taken turns in the shower, and he was settling in beside her. "I had no idea it would affect you that way."

She shook her head, making a vain attempt to hide her grin as she looked up at the wonderment in his face.

Dear Lord, had any man ever made her laugh more easily? she wondered, sobering. Had any man ever suited her better? Was there anyone she'd ever felt more attuned to, as if they'd been together forever? Was any face more precious to her? she pondered, reaching out to touch it lightly.

"It's less than four hundred miles away," he said gently, smiling with tenderness as he noticed the tears welling in her eyes. "I'll come with you if you want."

"There you go, being sweet again," she said, smiling in return, blinking away the tears, her heart aching as if she'd stubbed it against something in the dark, something hard and unexpected. "But I'll only be gone a day or two. Just long enough to make sure she's all right."

His hesitation was hardly noticeable before he asked, "Do you need any money?"

"Nope. I always have emergency plane fare. Thanks anyway."

He had his head propped up on one arm and was frowning down at her. "I wish you didn't look so lost. So sad. I'd feel better if I didn't think you were worried about her."

"I'm not. Truly. I just hate thinking of her being sick," she said, the lies seeming to come easier and easier now that she knew what had to be done. She needed to get away for a bit, to think, to make decisions, to plan. "She's hardly ever sick," she said, peppering the lies with tiny bits of truth to make herself feel better.

Oliver wasn't sure he wanted to believe her, but she'd always been so open with her feelings and thoughts, how could he not? He chose to believe he was imagining the pain and sorrow in her eyes and addressed himself to her expressed concerns.

"Then you should go and forget about everything here. The clinic won't fall apart while you're gone, and seeing her will make you feel better," he said. "Close your eyes and get some sleep now. We'll leave early and catch one of the commuter flights."

He stretched across her to reach the lamp switch. The room went suddenly dark. She couldn't see his face anymore and it frightened her.

"Oliver?"

"Hmmm?"

"Hold me really tight tonight, okay?"

"Okay," he said, taking her into his arms as he settled his large body against her slight form.

"No, I mean really tight. Like you won't ever let go."

"How's this? Better?"

"Perfect." Almost.

If she closed her eyes, she could almost believe he wouldn't let go, ever. She could almost pretend that she'd lie in his arms every night for the rest of her life, listening to gentle night noises; smiling at the sounds of their children stirring in their sleep; dozing contentedly, warm and happy; sleeping soundly, safe and blessed.

Almost . . . if she closed her eyes.

It wasn't yet dawn as she stood over the bed looking down on Oliver, his bare arm thrown limp across the sheets that no longer held her warmth. She hadn't closed her eyes once in those last hours with him. She hadn't believed and she couldn't pretend.

She locked the door on her way out, hoping he'd notice and know that she hadn't left him unprotected. She'd left a note saying she'd taken a cab to the airport, so he wouldn't worry. She'd resisted the urge to kiss him, so he wouldn't wake up and see her crying again.

For if it came to be that she was to bring pain and disillusionment to him, she didn't want her torment to be his last memory of her. No, because maybe, after some time and after some of the anger and hurt had faded, just maybe . . . he'd remember how she felt in his arms that night, and smile.

She ignored the Daly City train, took the Richmond/Fremont, and got off at the Berkeley station in time to get lost in the crowd of students who had returned after the Christmas holiday.

In her heart, she was on her way to L.A.; she was going home to Mama and the boys and the big old house on Chambrey Street—not the little motel wedged between a gas station and a convenience store off Ashby Avenue, that was really an OTE with the "M" and the "L" burnt out in the sign. As she sat in a corner of the dark little room in a straight-backed chair and cried, her heart dreamed of Mama pressing her head to her roomy soft lap, of her stroking her hair and listening patiently as she wept out her tale. In her heart, she twisted the large white handkerchief Mama always kept tucked away in her bodice, tightly in her fingers and closed her dry, scratchy eyes in relief. She felt herself being covered by the hand-stitched pink and white quilt that had been folded at the end of her bed for as long as she could remember. In her heart, she wasn't alone in a strange room, with dingy gray sheets and yellowed venetian blinds pulled flat against the daylight. In her heart, she had all the answers, still she cudgeled her brain with the hardest decision she'd ever made in her life. A decision with no winning answers. A decision she had to make for herself, for the clinic, for Oliver. A decision she had to make alone, one that not even Mama could help her with. . . .

Fifty-four hours later, Holly and her overnight bag sneaked out of the motel room. Locked inside the dull, dreary room, she left an innocent heart that was safer in the darkness, that wouldn't survive in the reality of a world where dreams didn't come true, where goodness didn't prevail and love didn't conquer all.

It was a silly old heart anyway, she determined, walking briskly to the BART station a few blocks away. It had been a naive heart that believed in the dignity and virtue of the human spirit, a heart that foolishly put its faith in mankind.

She was better off without it, she firmly decided, taking a seat on the train. Without a heart, decisions were easy . . . well, a little easier anyway. Without a heart to break, her dilemma had narrowed to a simple choice between her love for Oliver, and a multitude of needy people. She didn't need a heart to know what was expected of her, what her duty was, what was right and what was selfish.

What was the happiness of two people to the misery of thousands?

She walked home thinking it ironic that even love could be boiled down to a matter of dollars and cents. It was always money, and she hated it more now than she ever had before. Hated it, and couldn't help laughing contemptuously as she pulled two new overdrawn bank statements from her mailbox.

She looked up as she heard footsteps on the landing above.

"There you are!" Johanna exclaimed, as relieved as she was surprised to see her standing there. "Where have you been? I've been worried sick."

"Hi," Holly said, starting up the stairs toward her. She'd been hoping for more time to get used to her decision before she had to deal with any of the Careys. But it was becoming obvious that the Fates weren't going to cut her any slack this time.

"Where have you been?" Johanna asked again, clearly agitated and concerned.

"In a vacuum," she answered, and when Johanna frowned at her, she added, "Thinking."

"Oh, dear. What are you going to do?"

"What your mother wants," she said, trying not to rain her resentment down on the daughter. With each step her feet grew heavier, as if her shoes were magnets pulling the nails from the stairs. She was half-sick with exhaustion and miserable, and she didn't want to be back in her life again. She would have given everything she owned for sleeping pill and a little peace of mind. "She didn't leave me much of a choice."

"You can still tell Oliver, you know," Johanna said,

following her up to her apartment. "It's not too late. Tell him everything."

"I thought about it," she said, bending over the lock in the door with her key. "I was going to do it, too, but then I thought about you and her and Oliver. She's not his most favorite person in the world, I know, but she is all the family he has left. Her and you. I know what he'd do to her—and to you through her. I couldn't do it, Johanna," she said, letting them into her apartment and closing the door behind them. "Family is important, even if they are scumbags. No offense."

Johanna gave her a nervous smile. "Oliver wouldn't hold it against me. He knows I wouldn't hurt a fly, that I wouldn't . . . that I'm not capable of the things my mother can do. And I don't really think he'd miss her. You're much more important to him, Holly. He loves you."

"He does now, but family is family, and eventually he'd come to see that I'm the one who split his apart. I can't. And I can't take chances with the clinic either. Money's tight everywhere. We tried other foundations, the government, they're all stretched to their limits. We need the Carey Foundation—and your mother knows it."

Holly fell onto the couch and Johanna stood staring at her for a long time before she finally asked, "So, what happens next?"

Her head sagged back against the cushion, and she closed her eyes. She didn't want to open them ever again.

"I tear out Oliver's heart and have it for lunch while he watches. He's a pretty sharp guy. He'll get the picture, and your mother'll have what she wants."

"But how? What are you going to tell him?"

She rolled her head back and forth. "I have no idea."

"Don't you have a plan?"

She shrugged. "Who needs one? Oliver and I were doomed from the beginning. We're as suited for each other as a pair of male pit bulls. We're fascinated by our differences and we tolerate each other's views because we're in love, but we don't agree on anything. Any show of intolerance, any challenge or act of aggression will have us tearing each other's throats out in a matter of seconds."

"Are you sure it'll be that easy?" Johanna looked doubtful.

She looked at her then. "I never said it would be easy."

"Are you sure you're up to it? You look awful."

"How am I supposed to look?" she snapped, then regretted it. "Don't worry. The worse I look, the easier it'll be for him to leave me."

"Well, it's just that I think he's on his way over here now," she said, stepping to the window to look down into the street. "He knows you didn't go to L.A., and he somehow knew you'd be back today. He said it was Thursday and you never miss Thursdays." She sent a perplexed expression over her shoulder at Holly. "I assume you know what that means?"

She nodded, thinking of all the hair appointments she'd missed that day.

"How did he find out that I didn't go to L.A., do you know?"

"He called. Your foster mother said she hadn't seen

you since Thanksgiving and wasn't expecting you until after Easter."

She rolled and closed her eyes once more. "Well, if she wasn't sick before, she is by now—with worry," she said, with a sigh of remorse. She felt as if everything were turning to ash around her.

"Would you like some tea?" Johanna asked, her voice full of sympathy.

"No. Thanks," she said with a weak half-smile. "Maybe some coffee would help though. Want some? I'll make it."

"Sure," she said, turning to take another quick peek out the window. "But I'll make it. You don't look strong enough to—Oh, my goodness. Oh, Holly," she said, turning to look at her with an expression of panic and expectancy on her face.

"He's here?"

She nodded, and they stared at each other for a minute that lasted a year and a half.

Holly's lungs began to ache with the breath she was holding. It came out hard and fatalistically. She rubbed her face with her hands and started to rise to her feet.

"What about me?" Johanna whispered breathlessly.

"What?" she asked. Johanna wasn't the person looming in her mind. Johanna barely registered.

"Where can I go? Where can I hide? I shouldn't be here."

That was probably true. Johanna's presence would only complicate matters. Oliver might suspect that his family was involved in her decision to end their relationship, and then she'd never get rid of him.

She didn't want to be rid of him! Oh, Lord. It was her

heart. It had escaped. It was back and it was angry and hurt and screaming with indignation. To hell with the whole world, it shouted. Oliver was hers. He loved her. She loved him. What else could possibly be more important than that?

Through the exhaustion and quagmire of conflicting thoughts and emotions, Johanna's anxious fidgeting caught her attention.

"You stay here," she said, pulling herself together with no little effort. Standing, she clenched her teeth and refused to hear the clamor in her heart. "I'll head him off downstairs. I don't want him up here anyway. He won't make a scene in the streets."

"Don't be too sure of that," Johanna said, more at ease. "I don't think you realize what he's capable of."

"Maybe not," Holly said, grabbing up the jacket she'd just removed and heading for the door. "But if I don't let him up here, I won't have to throw him out. Where are you parked?"

"On the end of the block. That way," she said, pointing. "I parked on the side street. I was afraid he'd drive by and see my car."

"Good. When I get him out of the building, you come down and leave through the fire exit at the back."

She had to hurry. She thought she heard Johanna make a noise as she closed the door, as if she'd started to cry, but she didn't turn back to find out. She didn't care. The threat of her own tears concerned her more.

Her heart was frantic to get her attention. It was beating too fast and shooting pains through her chest. She turned her hands into fists, digging her nails into the palms to distract her mind from the aching in her chest, to focus it on the matter at hand . . . so to speak.

She'd made her decision. She'd considered everyone involved and made the best choice. Dashing down the second flight of stairs, she pressed her hand to her stomach as it lurched in hunger and chaos, threatening to revolt. She prayed for resolve and begged for the courage to do what had to be done. She conjured up mental pictures of the homeless families she'd encountered, the sick babies, the expressions of loss and bewilderment on the faces of men, women, and children of all ages—and hoped that the same expression on Oliver's face wouldn't kill her.

She yelped in surprise as she landed on the first floor and came face-to-face with Oliver, charging in through the doorway.

She swallowed hard and knew she looked guilty as hell as he glowered at her. She couldn't help it. She'd lied to him and he was angry. Who wouldn't feel guilty?

"Hi." She even sounded guilty, she thought. For little white lies about Marie Spoleto! She had big black whoppers yet to tell. She'd never pull it off if she didn't get a grip on herself.

"Well, hello," he said, with an impatient shift of his weight as he drew his arms akimbo, plainly expecting an explanation.

He was like nothing she could describe—big, mean, nasty, and royally teed off came to mind. And handsome. Sweet, caring, and gentle. Hurt and confused. She tried to swallow again but couldn't, her mouth was as dry as ancient dust in the pyramids.

"Your eyes look better," she said, her knees weak and trembling.

"Yours don't." His narrowed and studied her keenly. "They look like hell."

"Well, as a matter of fact, I haven't been sleeping well the past few days."

"Worried about Marie?"

"No. I . . ." Okay. She was just going to have to jump in and paddle as fast as she could. "I'm sorry about that, Oliver. I lied to you about her and I'm sorry for that, but I had to get away from you for a while and I didn't know how to come out and say so . . . so I lied."

His arms came slowly down to his sides as his eyes clouded over with a hurt and confusion that was worse than anything she'd imagined. She had to look away, and she couldn't bring herself to inflict another word upon him.

"I don't understand, Holly," he said in a quiet, controlled voice. "Why did you feel you needed to get away from me?"

It was now or never. The pain in his voice was like a double-edged razor, slashing at her heart in both directions with every word he uttered.

"Let's . . . let's go for a walk," she said impulsively, as the dark, drab walls of the small entry closed in around them. She took a tentative step forward, and when he didn't move, she said, "Please, Oliver, I need some air."

She brushed past him, and half-ran through the door and out into the cool January air like a prisoner escaping his guard, waiting to get shot in the back.

He followed quietly, glancing at her frequently and making a heroic effort to be patient with her.

"Oliver," she said, slowing and stopping on the sidewalk in front of the building. She turned to him. "I don't know how to say or do this tactfully, or without hurting you, so I . . ."

She couldn't do it. She loved him too much.

She had to do it. She loved him too much not to.

"I . . . I'll just say it straight out. I can't see you anymore."

"Why?" he asked quickly, as if it were the question he had prepared no matter what she'd said.

"We're too different. We want different things. And I feel as if you're smothering me."

"Smothering you?"

"Yes. I need time and space," she said, speaking directly to the buttons on his shirt. "I work all day, and when I come home I need space to think, time to be alone and recollect myself, put myself back together. I love what I do, but you have no idea what a drain it is on me. I give away little pieces of me all day, and then I come home and give more of myself to you and . . . and you deserve that, someone who can give you everything you want and need. But I get so tapped out, there just doesn't seem to be anything left of me, for me."

She took a peek at his face, and it was more than she could stand. She turned away and took several steps before his words stopped her.

"I don't mean to be dense, but just so I understand, are you choosing your job over our love?"

"Do you really think it's love, Oliver?" she asked, her eyes closed tightly.

"Yes."

She went on as if she hadn't heard him.

"I did some thinking about that, too, while I was gone. I mean, how do people know if they're in love or in serious lust? I wanted to go to bed with you the first time I saw you. Before I knew anything about you. What if all that's between us is just great sex?"

He grabbed her suddenly and spun her around so fast, her thoughts spun first in one direction, then in another.

"What are you doing?" he asked, his dark eyes nearly black with high emotions. He didn't mean to, but he was trembling so badly, he shook her. "Why are you doing this? What's happened?"

"Nothing's happened. Except that I suddenly felt lost, as if I'd wandered off the path I'd taken with my life and I couldn't find my way back. Then I realized that it was you. You were taking me in this new direction and . . . and . . ." She glanced up at his face. "Oh gawd, Oliver, I can't do this," she cried, tears spilling from her eyes as she lowered her head to his chest. "I can't. I'm selfish. I love you and I can't do this."

Now he was off the path, and he hadn't been too sure where it was leading him in the first place.

"Do what? What can't you do?"

"I can't send you away. I can't keep hurting you this way," she said, sobbing into the front of his ski jacket. "I'm sorry about all those people. I'm sorry about your family. I'm sorry I'm so selfish, but I can't do this. I love you. I can't even imagine what my life would be like without you. I . . . I don't want to imagine it. Oh, Oliver, I'm *so, so* sorry."

"Holly, honey," he stammered, beside himself with her tears and strange words. "You don't have to send me away. And you don't have to be sorry you love me. What is this?"

"I do. I do. I can't. But I should."

He pulled her away from him, realizing she was hysterical. He was tempted to slap her, but he couldn't bring himself to do it. Instead he shook her and shouted in her face.

"Holly! Stop this! Stop it now and tell me what's happened."

Her fists came up defensively, fearfully, between them. She blinked several times as she stared at him without seeing him.

"Oh, Oliver," she said, opening her hands to press the palms to his chest, as if to make sure he was really there, still there after all the horrible things she'd said to him. "Oliver, I didn't know what to do. I thought this was right but . . . it isn't. I don't want to hurt anyone, but I don't want to give you up either."

"You don't have to," he said emphatically. He was afraid to let go of her, but the tears on her cheeks were too compelling. He gently rubbed at them with the soft pad of his thumb. "Where is all this coming from?"

"Your aunt," she said, regretting the two words that would seal the woman's fate. She didn't like her, but she didn't wish her ill either. Furthermore, she knew that what she was about to say would hurt Oliver as well. "It was her idea."

"Elizabeth?"

She nodded. "I know you don't have much to do with the grants from the foundation, that you leave things pretty much to your aunt and the trustees. But you should know that both the clinic and St. Augustine's operate off large grants from the Carey Foundation."

"I know that," he said, taking his turn to nod, even though he was still puzzled.

"You knew?"

"Sure. Phil Rosenthal told me about St. Augustine's the night of the costume party. And, of course, I checked on the clinic before I made the personal donation before Christmas. What made you think I didn't know about the grants?"

"I asked you. The night we made love, the night you were angry. I asked if you gave the money to the clinic because of me, and you said I was the one who'd drawn your attention to it."

"And you were. I wouldn't have checked on the grants otherwise."

"But the review notice came the same day as your donation. I couldn't imagine that you'd be giving us money and trying to take it away at the same time."

"I wasn't. I was just making a contribution. Elizabeth initiated the review."

"Well, that's what I thought. I knew she didn't like me much, and I was afraid she'd refuse to renew it if she knew I was connected with the clinic, and then when Jo—"

"But Elizabeth did know you were connected with the clinic," he said, cutting off the end of her sentence. "She came to me and asked if I knew about it, and when I said I did, she suggested a fifteen percent increase in the grant."

"She did?"

"Yes. And she told me that she'd suggested the review

to the committee and that it was very clear to everyone that the clinic needed more funding."

"She did?"

"Yes. I was there when she called her secretary and told her to start the paperwork for the new grant and to schedule a hearing to present it the clinic and to tell you and your friend Joan Ellerbey in person how pleased they were with your efforts."

"Really? When was this?"

He shrugged and tried to think of the exact date.

"I don't remember. Sometime after Christmas. She felt awful that she hadn't connected your name to the clinic until then and wondered if you'd been offended that she hadn't."

"But . . ." She stopped, glancing up to the windows of her apartment and then down the street as new questions began to burn in her brain.

"But what?"

"Does Johanna have any connection with the Carey Foundation?"

"Johanna? No. What's she got to do with this?"

"I don't know. She's been coming to see me. To warn me about your aunt."

"She's been coming here?" His cousin was strictly an uptown girl; imagining her in Oakland was almost impossible for him. "Are you telling me that all this was Johanna's idea? She told you to dump me?"

"Yes," she said slowly. "But I thought it was coming from your aunt."

Briefly, she told him everything Johanna had said and done in her presence since the Christmas party at his home, including their conversation in the powder room that night.

"I don't understand," he said, shaking his head. "Why would she want to do this?" He was thoughtful for a moment. "She was always kind of a mean kid, I know. She used to come home from school and con me into taking her someplace, and then she'd steal things, break stuff, pick fights with guys that I'd have to finish for her. Then she'd invariably blame everything on me so she wouldn't get into trouble and get shipped back to school early or off to some summer camp." He shrugged. "And I'd never bother to deny it, because no one would have believed me anyway, with my record, and I . . . I always felt sort of sorry for her, in a way. I mean, I think I understood that she had her problems, too, in those days."

"So, this was just one of Johanna's pranks?"

"Pretty sick for a prank, don't you think?" he asked. "I think it's *really* sick. Disturbed even."

She glanced up at her apartment windows again, remembering the woman she'd left up there. Sweet, gentle, friendly, caring Johanna.

Oliver followed her gaze to the windows.

"Is she up there now? Is she waiting for you to come back?"

He was halfway to the door before she could stop him.

"No. She's gone. She was here when I got home. She came to warn me that you knew I'd been lying about going to L.A. and that you were on your way over here. I told her to go out the back way once I got you out of the building and to go home. I'm sure she did. She was terrified that you'd catch her here." She hesitated. "Oliver, she wanted me to tell you the whole story. She wanted me to tell you what your aunt was planning. Are you sure it was Johanna playing the tricks and not your aunt?"

"I'm sure," he said. "People like you are easy targets for people like her. She could read you like a book. She knew you'd be too proud to tell me at first, that you'd want to fight your own battle with my aunt rather than ask me to intervene for you. If she knew about Carolann and how you felt about Marie, she'd also know the high value you give to family. She knew you'd never tell me."

"But why? Why the elaborate plan? Why would she want to hurt us so much?"

"Who knows? I never could guess what went on in her head."

"What do you suppose'll happen when she finds out it didn't work this time? What'll she do when she finds out I couldn't go through with it?"

"We're not waiting to find out what she's going to do," he said, taking hold of her shoulders. "I want you to go back upstairs, lock your door, and try to get some sleep before you walk out in the middle of traffic and get yourself killed. You look awful, sweetheart."

"That's what Johanna said." Her smile was a weak one. "What are you going to do?"

"Catch up with her and get to the bottom of all this," he said. He pushed a few wayward hairs out of her face with gentle fingers. "Then I'll kill her for putting you through this."

"Bring her back and I'll kill her myself," she said, knowing they were speaking in the abstract. She walked him to his car and returned his quick kiss, then watched as he let a car pass by before moving around to the driver's side.

"Oliver?"

He looked over the top of the car at her.

"Can you forgive me? For what I just put you through? I let her influence me. I know . . . that I hurt you. I'm as much to blame as she is for that."

He smiled, and she saw the forgiveness in his eyes, even as he said, "I'm not sure yet. You and I are going to have a really long discussion later, about trust and being too damned independent. We'll see how repentant you are then."

She grinned her never-fail grin. "I was raised with Catholics, remember? I have penance down to a fine art."

He laughed and declared that he'd be doing the judging in this case. He took a few seconds to enjoy the sound of her laughter, then got in his car and drove away. She watched him take the corner at the end of the block and vanish, then turned back toward her apartment building.

TWELVE

This time she took the stairs two at a time. She felt jet propelled. Life was good. She'd just won the lottery, and the grand prize was happily ever after. Yes, Holly, there is a Santa Claus, she decided, feeling giddy and whimsical as she topped the stairs and crossed to her apartment door. A Santa Claus, an Easter Bunny, a tooth fairy, and a . . .

. . . boogeyman. She stopped short just inside the door, her blood running hot and then cold and then hot again.

"Johanna," she said, forcing a smile to her lips as she struggled to keep her eyes off the small, nasty-looking gun in the woman's hand. She recognized the silencer on it from television.

In the split second it had taken her to identify the deadly weapon, she'd noticed for the first time that Johanna's hands were small with long, elegant fingers. The observation was somehow just as unsettling as finding her still in the apartment and holding a gun.

"Hi. I'm glad you're still here," she said, hoping her voice sounded as calm and unperturbed as Johanna looked. She needed time to think, and stepping behind an illusion of normalcy was her only chance. "I was afraid you'd already left."

"Were you?" One carefully plucked brow lifted in mild surprise.

"Uh-huh. I'm afraid I was rude earlier, and I wanted a chance to apologize—and to thank you for all your help."

"You were rude," she agreed passively. "You snapped at me."

"I know. I'm sorry," she said, gauging the distance between them, wondering if she could overpower her—or would it be wiser to turn and make a run for it through the open door behind her? "I was tired and upset, but that's no excuse for biting your head off."

"I forgive you," she said, her smile charming and friendly.

"Thanks. Would you like that coffee now? Or tea? We can sit and talk."

She took a step toward the kitchen, but Johanna stopped her with her words.

"Did you tell him?"

Holly glanced from Johanna to the window with the sudden realization that she had been watching.

"Of course I did. You watched. You saw how hurt and angry he was, didn't you?"

A frown of confusion furrowed her pretty face. Her gaze darted to the window, hit the floor, then bounced back to Holly.

"I saw that, but then you started to cry and he wasn't angry anymore. What else did you tell him?"

"I couldn't help crying, it wasn't easy for me," she said, hoping she was showing enough shame and pain in her eyes to be convincing. "And . . . and I didn't think Oliver would believe me if I was coldhearted and brutal about it. So when I started to cry, it seemed only natural to try to convince him that we could still be friends if he wanted, but that was all I could give him. And . . . and you could see he wasn't real keen on that, so then we talked some more. I told him he was suffocating me and that I had a plan for my life that . . ." serendipitously, tears came to her eyes with the recollection, ". . . that didn't involve him."

"And that convinced him?" Johanna didn't look wholly convinced herself.

"Well, I said other things; I can't remember all of it," she said, wiping the tears from her eyes. "But, yes, I think in the end, he could see that it was over for us."

"He wasn't angry when he left."

"No. Bewildered and trying to hang on to his pride, but not angry," she said, sounding a little testy herself. "Not yet, anyway. I think it happened so suddenly that it shocked him. The angry part won't hit him till later. I need a drink. You want one?"

Johanna allowed her to walk into the kitchen, which amazed Holly. She was frightened and horrified, but not yet terrified to the point of nonthinking. Instantly she started looking for a weapon of her own.

"What if he comes back?" she heard her ask. "What will you do then?"

"I'll send him away. I don't need the kind of trouble your mother can give me."

"What about after you have the grant? Will you take him back?"

Quietly opening and closing drawers and cupboards, all she'd been able to come up with were knives—not much use against a gun unless she could get close enough.

"Did you want a drink?"

"No. What about after you get the grant? Will you take him back?"

She sloshed red wine into a glass and hurriedly returned to the living room with it—the biggest knife in her arsenal tucked carefully into the back of her jeans.

"Why would he want to come back?" she asked morosely, leaning against a wall. "He's a proud man. He won't come back to where he's not wanted. Not when he can have any woman he wants, who wants him in return."

Johanna seemed to be thinking this over, then she smiled and agreed, "Like me, for instance?"

"You?"

"Don't look so surprised, Holly." There was a sharp edge to her voice, even though her facial expression remained sweet and angelic. "Oliver and I were always meant to be together. As a matter of fact, that's why my mother had to die, my real mother. She had to die so that Daddy could marry Elizabeth and then I could be with Oliver, forever."

"I . . . I didn't know Elizabeth wasn't your birth mother."

"Yes you did. I told you we were related only by marriage, that I was as much a candidate for Oliver's affections as anyone else."

Holly shook her head. She could vaguely recall the

words now, but she hadn't made the connection at the time.

"And Elizabeth was never any kind of mother to me," she went on. "She made Daddy send me away to school. And if I got into any kind of trouble at all when I came home, she made him send me away again. To my aunt Corrinne's in Southampton or to visit my mother's sister, Jessica, in South Carolina. She never wanted me around. She was always afraid that Oliver would fall in love with me and make his father unhappy."

For a second, Holly imagined she heard movement on the stairs outside her door, and in the hallway. Her heart fluttered with relief. If she could get someone's attention and stall Johanna long enough for someone to get help. . . . She spoke quickly to conceal the noise from Johanna.

"Why, uh, why would Oliver's falling in love with you make his father unhappy?" she asked.

"He never liked my daddy. He didn't think he was good enough for his precious sister, Elizabeth. He hated me too. He was in on it with Elizabeth, sending me away all the time, sending me away from Oliver so he couldn't fall in love me. They always kept Oliver home, but me they sent away."

"Maybe . . ." she stalled. "Maybe they would have sent Oliver away, too, if he wasn't such a bad boy? Maybe they didn't think it was safe to send him away?"

"He was never really a bad boy," she said, smiling. "All he ever needed was someone to love him. I think that deep down he knew I loved him. But they kept sending me away, and he would rebel. It was only natural.

I don't think even Oliver knew why he was doing all those things he used to do."

"No. He probably . . . didn't," she stammered, as Oliver's large form filled the doorway. The door blocked the view between him and Johanna. She couldn't see him, and he couldn't see that she had a gun. Now Holly was terrified. "You know, Johanna," she said impulsively, turning a bit to set her glass on the table, hoping beyond reason that Oliver would catch sight of the knife in her waistband, guess at the situation, and go for help. "Adults do so many unthinking, unfeeling things to children. They run around living their own lives and never think about what it's doing to their children. Look at me and Carolann. She was *crazy,*" she said, emphasizing the word for Oliver's sake. "Using all those drugs. She might as well have put a *gun* to her head, for all the good it did her . . . and me."

Johanna made a regretful grimace.

"Yours is a sad story, too, Holly. And I'm sorry for that. I liked you. I thought you had a lot of potential. You could have made something of your life if you'd been given a chance."

She felt the ominous change as her life slipped from the present to the past tense as Johanna spoke. Her fingers started to ache and her palms were clammy. Her heart was throbbing in her throat, and tears were backing up behind her eyes. Johanna was planning to kill her. She knew it as well as she knew that Oliver was still at the door, that he hadn't yet gone for help, that her time was running out.

"Why are you doing this, Johanna?" she asked quietly, not wishing to disturb her serene disposition. "I thought we were friends. I trusted you. I did everything you asked of me. I sent Oliver away. I didn't confront your mother. Why this? Why the gun?"

"Like I said, yours is a sad story. You were always going to die, whether you sent Oliver away or not. You were always going to be another statistic, another poor young woman shot and killed in her own apartment. This really is a terrible neighborhood, Holly."

"But why? I haven't hurt you." Her peripheral vision caught Oliver motioning her back. Back toward the bathroom or the kitchen? The kitchen would put Johanna's back to Oliver—if she followed. "I won't hurt you. I'm your friend."

"I don't have friends," she said simply. "I have people who like me because they think I have money, but no real friends. I'll be sorry to lose you, Holly. I'll cry when I read about it in the papers. I'll cry on Oliver's shoulder at your funeral. And I'll be sorry. I truly will be, but you couldn't have stayed here. I've seen the way Oliver looks at you. He never would have given up. He would have been hurt and then angry for a couple of weeks, during which time you would have been brutally killed, of course, but then I thought that as long as I was here . . ." She shrugged and the gun in her hand wavered unsteadily. "I mean, why come all the way back?"

"Johanna," she said, her tone reasoning. She took a tiny, baby step back toward the kitchen, and Oliver stepped to one side of the door, still watching and listening intently. "You don't want to do this." She took another minute step backward. "You've never killed anyone before, and . . . and I hear it's really ugly." Another small step. "I hear it's something that lives with you forever, that never leaves your mind. I hear it haunts you. You don't want something like that to ruin your life with Oliver, do you?" One more shaky step. Her heart jumped when Johanna took one forward. "I . . . uh . . . I'll move away. I'll leave. I'll disappear, out of Oliver's life."

"What about your mother?"

"Who? Carolann? I'll take her with me. I'll transfer her to another facility. I can do that. I'm her legal guardian, you know."

She'd taken three more small steps. Johanna had taken two. The apartment felt as big as the Taj Mahal. She was beginning to think she'd never reach the kitchen. Then she felt the doorway behind her.

She must have looked surprised or relieved or glad that she'd reached the opening, because Johanna smiled at her with great sympathy and understanding. "Please don't make this any harder than it has to be, Holly."

Without looking, she reached out and pushed at the open door. Only Holly saw Oliver's fingers suddenly gripping the jamb to keep it from closing completely.

"Hiding in the kitchen won't help, you know." Her laughter was pleasant and unnaturally natural. "A liberated woman like you wouldn't want to die in the kitchen anyway. No. You deserve better. You should die like a real heroine. Burned at the stake or . . . well, how do they kill heroines these days?" She paused. "I do admire you, Holly. You're everything I always wanted to be. You have everything I always wanted. And Oliver. Don't you see that I can't let you stay?"

Holly shook her head. She couldn't see it. And she'd run out of words. Her breath came in ragged gasps, and the tears finally broke loose and began to trickle down her cheeks. She was no heroine, she thought, as she questioned the wisdom of falling to her knees and begging for her life.

She stumbled back into the kitchen and found herself pressed tight against the counter, next to the sink. Johanna took one last step to point the gun directly at her. There was nowhere else to go. No place to hide.

The door to the hall swung open, and Oliver's face was both heavenly and devilish. Tight. Focused. Malevolent. Holly averted her gaze to keep from telegraphing his presence to Johanna.

"You'll see. This is best for all of us, Holly," she was saying. "Maybe you should turn around. It'll be easier for you if you don't watch."

"E-easier for you too," she stammered, taking her last stubborn stand. She looked straight into her eyes. "So you won't have to see. I want you to see, Johanna. I won't let you forget what you're doing."

Johanna cocked her head to one side, as if struck by a sudden notion. She smiled. She raised her hand slightly, taking careful aim.

At Holly's head! Don't shoot me in the head, she kept thinking. Mama won't recognize me. Oliver will be disgusted. Not my face. Not my head. Not my mind.

They all heard it at the same time. Oliver had taken several steps into the room and was within reach of Johanna's arm when his final step disturbed the aged floorboard beneath his foot. It whined and squeaked as if it were in pain; a noise generally unnoticed or ignored was now louder than the screams from hell.

The next second crawled by in the space of an eternity.

Johanna turned, the gun aimed straight at Oliver's heart. Holly screamed and took a mad, wild dive at Johanna from behind. Oliver ducked out of the way even as he tried to reach out and grab the gun. When the gun fired, with so quiet and benign a sound, like a rush of air that was heard and gone in the same instant, no one even realized it had gone off. But suddenly there was blood, and the three of them grappled for the gun. The blood, the horror, the screams, the grunts, the cries . . .

And then it was over.

The clocks started again and time moved on.

The gun fell to the floor and Johanna broke loose, knocking Oliver to one side and down to his knees, dropping Holly to the floor behind her. She'd vanished through the door before Holly could look up, and then all she saw was Oliver's blood—on the wall behind him, on the floor, on his face. Part of the left sleeve of his ski jacket was missing.

"Oliver!" she cried as he got to his feet and turned to follow Johanna. "Oliver! You're hurt. Stop!"

"Call the police," he shouted back at her with what seemed like his last breath. "Now! Stay here. Wait for me."

"What?"

"Stay here. Wait for me." He repeated his words from several feet down the hall.

Holly staggered over to the telephone. It was so queer. . . . The entire incident with Johanna didn't seem nearly as strange to her as Oliver's parting words. Not the "stay here," but the "wait for me" words. They rang like bells in the back of her head as she dialed 911.

"Wait for me. Wait for me. Wait for me."

She disengaged the "please hold" and redialed.

"Wait for me. Wait for me." The words were *so* familiar, and yet she was sure he'd never said them to her before. It was like . . . like a dream, like a memory . . . like déjà vu, or simply a mental souvenir to jog her memory of some great event or precious moment.

When the operator answered, she quickly told her the information she needed and then dashed to the door to follow Oliver, without hanging up the phone.

She found him, with Johanna wrapped tightly in his arms, on the stairs below the second-floor landing. She couldn't tell if there had been a struggle. Johanna was weeping pitifully, and he was rocking her back and forth, and back and forth, looking dazed, weak, and tired.

He heard her on the stairs above them and looked up. There was a sadness in his eyes that came directly from his soul. A little relief, too, some remorse and some pity. There was blood soaking through the hole in the left sleeve of his jacket, and she could see that his left hand was covered with it—it was dripping off one side.

"Oliver," she said, whispering and not knowing why as she crouched and crept closer to them. "Your arm . . ."

He shook his head and closed his eyes without loosening his grip on Johanna. His head jerked upright and he opened his eyes again, as if he'd almost fallen asleep.

"I called," she said quietly, talking to keep him awake; to keep him from passing out from the shock and the pain and the loss of blood. "They'll be here soon. Hold on, Oliver. Is she all right? Is she hurt?"

He glanced down at his step-cousin, frowning as if he didn't know who she was, then shook his head.

"I don't think so," he murmured. After a moment, he added, "I never dreamed . . . I saw her car . . . down the street . . . I never thought . . ."

"No one did." She heard sirens in the distance, and for the first time in her life, she welcomed the familiar sound, praying they were headed their way. "It's over. All her pain is out in the open now, and she can begin to heal."

"Why didn't I see it?" he asked, his voice low and frail. "I never looked at her. I never saw her."

"You had to heal your own wounds first, Oliver. It isn't anyone's fault."

His head sort of bobbed on his shoulders, and he tightened his hold on Johanna. She lay in his arms like a loose bag of bones. Powerless. Without purpose. She wept quietly now, her sobbing muffled in his ski jacket.

Wanting to cry, not for Johanna, not for Oliver, not for herself, but for the whole world, Holly closed her eyes and leaned the side of her head against the stairwell. The three of them were safe now. Not from one another, but from their pasts.

Not a cynic by nature, she couldn't help but wonder who the fool was who had made babies the symbol of new life, of new beginnings. There ought to be someone around to point at, to tell them they were wrong, to show them how children come into the world carrying the baggage of their parents.

Kind, loving baggage from Marie and Roberto Spoleto. Deluded and pathetic, maybe, well-intended baggage from Carolann and whoever her father was. Quiet, misguided baggage from Oliver's parents. Selfish, greedy, mindless baggage from Max and Elizabeth George.

Good or bad, it was all baggage that children had no control over. All they could do was take it in and react to it. Was it a dice roll, a flip of the coin, a draw of the straw as to whose suitcase they ended up with? Or did it all fit into her theory of reincarnation as to whether you got nice sturdy, dependable luggage or a beat-up knapsack at birth? Either way, it was plain that a baby's life was never truly fresh and new. It was more an extension of the life it came from, and the life before that, and the one before that. . . .

A child's life was never his own until he accepted the burden of his parents' belongings and molded them into something he could carry and live with. And then . . . he passed to his child, and to his child after that, and to his child after that . . .

THIRTEEN

The police took Johanna away.

Holly protested when they handcuffed her; it was like watching them bind up a Raggedy Ann doll. But they insisted it was as much for her own protection as it was for theirs, and they were gentle with her as they passed her into the backseat of the squad car.

She'd stopped crying. She sat mute and staring off into space as if it were happening to someone else. As if she weren't really there at all.

"Johanna?" Holly said softly, leaning into the car, a policeman standing nearby. "Johanna? If you can hear me, I want you to know this doesn't change anything. I still want to be your friend."

The woman's blue eyes moved slowly toward hers, but when they met, there was no sign of Johanna in them.

"I understand, Johanna. I know and I understand."

Johanna didn't care.

She stepped back and closed the door, and as she watched the car drive away she thought of Carolann.

How many times had she been taken away in just such a manner? And how many times had she fought her way back, only to find that there was still no one around to tell her they loved her?

It wouldn't happen to Johanna. Johanna had Holly—and Holly knew about love.

An ambulance had been called for Oliver.

He'd passed into unconsciousness almost the minute the policemen had pried his fingers loose of Johanna. He'd come around momentarily, to protest their prodding fingers near his wound and to insist that an ambulance wouldn't be necessary if they'd give him a ride to a hospital, and then he was gone again.

Holly held his head in her lap until the paramedics came. She answered the policemen's questions and told them to contact Oliver's aunt in regard to both Oliver and Johanna. In the end, she'd made the entire incident sound more like a family dispute with the gun going off by accident—which in truth it had—and not like the intended murder it might have been.

She followed the stretcher they'd put Oliver on into the back of the ambulance and held his hand as they drove away from the apartment building. She wondered briefly if anyone had thought to close her front door, but didn't think of it again as Oliver began to stir to consciousness once more.

"Holly?"

"Yes, Oliver. I'm here."

"Don't go away."

"I won't, Oliver. I'll be right here."

"Wait for me."

Aw, wow. There it was again. All the little hairs on

her arms and at the back of her neck stood straight up and wiggled with the heebie-geebies.

"You aren't going anywhere, Oliver. Just to the hospital, and I'll stay with you the whole time. I promise."

"Wait for me."

"I will. Stop saying that. I promise, I will," she said. She was almost shouting at him. He didn't seem to be hearing her reassurances. "Oliver?"

He'd lapsed into unconsciousness once more. He was so pale. He was always so strong and confident; it was frightening to see him helpless and weak. What if the paramedics were wrong? What if it was more than what they'd called a simple flesh wound? What if he'd lost more blood than they suspected? What kind of a gunshot wound was ever simple, for crying out loud?

"Oliver?" she called, recognizing the panic in her own voice.

Panic that hadn't been there the whole time she'd been with Johanna. Panic that hadn't been there when she'd talked to the police. Panic that wouldn't be there at all if it hadn't suddenly occurred to her how close she'd come to losing him, how close to his heart the bullet had come, how close to her heart he'd become.

"Oliver, don't die," she said, starting to cry at last. She slid off whatever she was sitting on, elbowed the attendant out of the way, and got closer to him. "Please, Oliver," she said close to his ear. "We can be rich if you want. You can buy me a car, a big one, a big red one, and I'll drive it everywhere. . . . And a house, bigger than Carey House, with gold door-knockers and . . . and bodyguards." She sniffed and wiped her cheek and nose with the back of her hand. "Big, ugly bodyguards. You can buy me anything you want and I'll act happy to get it, even if I don't need it, and . . . and in the winter we'll burn the money. I'll roll ten-dollar bills into little Pres-to-Logs"—she showed him how she'd do it with her fingers—"and we'll take turns throwing them into the fireplace, just please, please don't die."

"Ma'am?" said the medic beside her. She glanced at him. He was watching her as if he thought she needed the stretcher more than Oliver did. "Ma'am, he isn't going to die. His vital signs are stable and he's stopped bleeding. He's just weak. He'll be fine."

"Oh, what do you know?" she said irrationally. "People die all the time when they're not supposed to. I did and look at me."

He was. With a great deal of caution.

"Holly?" It was Oliver. His voice was weak; his lips were dry.

"Yes, Oliver? Oh, yes, Oliver, what?"

He opened his eyes, but he had to tip his head a bit to see her.

"Don't cry anymore. I can't stand it."

"Okay. I won't cry anymore." She hastily wiped her cheeks dry.

"And will you do me a favor?"

"Anything, Oliver."

"Don't ever change who you are, okay? Not for me. Not for anyone."

"No. I won't."

"And Holly? One more thing?"

"What?"

"Will you marry me, before you burn all my money?"

❖————————❖

It would be many years yet before Oliver told his wife about the strange dreams he had after he was shot that afternoon. Weird yet pleasing dreams that would return now and again in the night and cause him to wake and ponder life and the universe beyond.

Nimbus sort of dreams, clouded and light, with no faces or entities, but with voices that were as real and familiar to him as hers was as she promised tearfully to love him, honor him, and spend all his money.

Secret sort of dreams, the kind you're afraid to talk about before breakfast, because they might come true if you do. And it wasn't that the dreams were so terrible, it was just that they sometimes felt more real to him than certain parts of his life.

Deep-seated dreams. They were rooted firmly in both his conscious and subconscious mind and triggered by external stimuli—usually Holly. The simplest things would call them to mind . . . Holly with her hands on her hips and a frown on her face, saying, "There you are. I couldn't find you anywhere." Or Holly halfway up the stairs to their bedroom, her eyes bright with desire and her lips whispering, "Hurry." Or Holly coming home two hours late with a child in each hand, her hair standing on end, as she complained, "I got lost. I took the wrong exit. I was completely lost."

And always, always, it would be on the tip of his tongue to tell her, "Wait for me."

THE EDITOR'S CORNER

The end of summer means back to school and cooler weather, but here at LOVESWEPT temperatures are rising with four sensational romances to celebrate the beginning of autumn. You'll thrill to the sexiest heroes and cheer for the most spirited heroines as they discover the power of passion. They're sure to heat up your reading hours with their wonderful, sensuous tales.

Leading our lineup is the marvelously talented Debra Dixon with **MOUNTAIN MYSTIC,** LOVESWEPT # 706. Joshua Logan has always been able to read anyone's emotions, but he can't figure Victoria Bennett out—maybe because his longing for the beautiful midwife is so unexpected! He'd come home to the mountains seeking refuge from a world that demanded more than he could give; why now did he have to meet a woman who awakened his need to touch and be touched? Debra weaves a moving story of trust and healing that you won't forget.

Donna Kauffman invites you to meet a **BOUNTY HUNTER,** LOVESWEPT # 707. Kane Hawthorne was hired to locate a runaway wife, but when he finds Elizabeth Lawson, he knows he has to claim her as his own! A desperate woman who dares trust no one, she tries to keep him from making her enemies his, but Kane insists on fighting her demons. And she has no choice but to cherish her savage hero until his own ghosts are silenced. With this electrifying romance Donna proves that nobody does it better when it comes to writing about a dangerous and sexy man.

Cindy Gerard's newest book will keep you awake long **INTO THE NIGHT,** LOVESWEPT # 708. It began as a clever gimmick to promote a radio show for lovers, but the spirited sparring between Jessie Fox and Tony Falcone is so believable, listeners demand to know more of their steamy romance! Jessie vows it is impossible for this gorgeous younger man to want her with the fire she sees burning in his eyes —until the brash Falcon sets a seductive trap his Fox can't escape. Cindy's irresistible blend of humor and playful passion creates a memorable couple you will cherish.

The ever popular Peggy Webb has written her most sensual and heartbreaking novel yet with **ONLY HIS TOUCH,** LOVESWEPT # 709. For years Kathleen Shaw's body had danced to the music of Hunter La Farge's mouth and hands, but when the beautiful ballerina loses everything she'd lived for in a shocking accident, the untamed adventurer is the last man she wants to face. Twice before he'd lost the woman who shared his soul, but now the fierce panther who had claimed her for all time must set her free to recapture her dream. This is Peggy at her best —keep a box of tissues handy!

I'd like to take this opportunity to share with you some exciting news. I have been promoted to Deputy Publisher here at Bantam and will consequently be managing all aspects of the Bantam adult hardcover, trade, and mass-market paperback publishing program. I will continue to oversee women's fiction, but most of the hands-on work will be handled by Senior Editor Beth de Guzman, Assistant Editor Shauna Summers, and Administrative Editor Gina Iemolo. Of course, none of this changes our team's continuing goal to bring you the best in contemporary romantic fiction written by the most talented and loved authors in the genre.

Happy reading!

With warmest wishes,

Nita Taublib

Nita Taublib

Deputy Publisher

P.S. Don't miss the exciting women's novels from Bantam that are coming your way in September— **ADAM'S FALL** is the paperback reprint of the classic romantic novel from *New York Times* bestselling author Sandra Brown; **THE LAST BACHELOR,** from nationally bestselling author Betina Krahn, is a spectacularly entertaining battle of the sexes set in Victorian England; **PRINCE OF WOLVES,** by Susan Krinard, is a spellbinding new romance of mystery, magic, and forbidden passion in the tradition of Linda Lael Miller; and **WHISPERED LIES** is the latest novel from Christy Cohen, about two intimate strangers divided by dangerous secrets, broken vows, and misplaced passions. We'll be giving you a sneak peek at these terrific books in next month's LOVE-SWEPTs. And immediately following this page look for a preview of the exciting romances from Bantam that are *available now!*

Don't miss these electrifying books by
your favorite Bantam authors

On sale in July:
MIDNIGHT WARRIOR
by Iris Johansen

BLUE MOON
by Luanne Rice

VELVET
by Jane Feather

WITCH DANCE
by Peggy Webb

Iris Johansen

THE *NEW YORK TIMES* BESTSELLING
AUTHOR OF
THE BELOVED SCOUNDREL

MIDNIGHT WARRIOR

From the author who has been lauded as "the Mistress of Romantic Fantasy" comes a passionate new tale of danger, adventure, and romance that sweeps from a Saxon stronghold to a lovers' bower in the cool, jade-green forests of Wales. . . .

Brynn hesitated for a moment and then said reluctantly, "This is a bad place. Can't you feel it?"

"Feel what?"

"If you cannot feel it, I can't explain. I just want to be gone from here." She paused and then whispered, "Please."

He looked at her in surprise. "This must mean a good deal to you. You're more given to commands than pleas."

She didn't answer.

"What if I give you what you wish?" He lowered his voice to silky softness. "Will you give me a gift in turn?"

"I've given you a gift. Your friend Malik is alive. Isn't that enough for you?"

"It should be."

"But it isn't?"

"Malik will tell you I don't know the meaning of enough. The prize just over the horizon is always the sweetest."

"So you reach out and take it," she said flatly.

"Or barter for it. I prefer the latter. It suits my merchant's soul. I suppose Malik has told you that I'm more trader than knight?"

"No, he said you were the son of a king and capable of being anything you wanted to be."

"Which obviously did not impress you."

"Why should it? It does not matter their station, men are all the same."

He smiled. "Certainly in some aspects. You didn't answer. Will you barter with me?"

"I have nothing with which to barter."

"You're a woman. A woman always has great bartering power."

She straightened her shoulders and turned to look directly at him. "You mean you wish me to be your whore."

His lips tightened. "Your words lack a certain delicacy."

"They do not lack truth." She looked down into the pot. "You wish me to part my limbs and let you rut like a beast of the forest. I wonder you even seek to bargain. You think me your slave. Isn't a slave to be used?"

"Yes," he said curtly. "A slave is to work and give

pleasure. And you're right, I don't have to bargain with you. I can do what I wish."

"I'm glad that is clear." She stirred faster, harder. "Shall we go into the tent now? Or perhaps you wish to take me in front of all your soldiers? I'd be grateful if you'd have the kindness to let me finish preparing this salve that is making your friend well and healthy. But if I seem unreasonable, you must only tell me and I will—"

"Be silent!" His teeth clenched, he added, "I've never met a woman with such a—"

"I'm only being humble and obliging. Isn't that what you want of me?"

"I want—" He stopped and then said thickly, "I'm not certain what I want . . . yet. When I do, I'll be sure you're made fully aware of it."

"Rice has an elegant style, a sharp eye and a real warmth. In her hands families—and their values—seem worth cherishing."
—*San Francisco Chronicle*

BLUE MOON

BY

Luanne Rice

BLUE MOON is a moving novel of a family that discovers the everyday magic of life and the extraordinary power of love. The New York Times *has already praised it as "a rare combination of realism and romance."* Entertainment Weekly *has simply called it "brilliant," and* People *has raved that it is "eloquent . . . a moving and complete tale of the complicated phenomenon we call family."*

Here is a look at this powerful novel. . . .

After two weeks at sea, Billy Medieros was heading home. He usually loved this part of the trip, when the hold was full of fish and his crew was happy because they knew their share of the catch would be high, and they'd all sleep in their own beds that night. He drove the *Norboca*—the best boat in his father-in-law's fleet—around Minturn Ledge, and Mount Hope came into view.

Billy stood at the wheel. The tide had been against

him, and he knew he had missed Cass. She would have left work by now, was probably already home cooking supper. He could picture her at the stove, stirring something steamy, her summer dress sticking damply to her breasts and hips. His wife had the body of a young sexpot. Other guys at sea would pray to Miss July, but Billy would look at pictures of Cass, her coppery curls falling across her face, her blue eyes sexy and mysterious, delicate fingers cupping her full breasts, offering them to the camera. She had given him a Minolta for his last birthday, but for his real present she had posed nude.

Lately, to Billy, Cass had seemed more real in his bunk at sea than she was at home. In person, Cass looked the same, she smelled the same, but she seemed absent, somehow. Raising Josie changed her every day, and Billy resisted the transformation. He missed his wife.

He was nearly home. His eyes roved the church spires, the wooden piers clawing the harbor, American flags flapping from the yacht club and every hotel roof, white yachts rocking on the waves, two trawlers heading out. He waved to the skippers, both of whom he had fished with before. Manuel Vega waved back, a beer in his hand.

Billy couldn't stand skippers who drank onboard. It set a bad example for the crew. You had to stay keen every second. Billy had seen terrible things happen to fishermen who weren't paying attention—fingers lost to a winch handle, a skull split open by a boom. On Billy's first trip out with his father-in-law, Jimmy Keating, a crewmate with both hands busy setting nets had bitten down on a skinny line to hold it in place, and a gust of wind had yanked out six of his top teeth.

Stupid. Billy had no patience for stupid crew

members, and dulling your senses with alcohol, at sea on a fifty-foot boat, was stupid.

"Docking!" Billy yelled, and four guys ran up from below. John Barnard, Billy's first mate for this trip, stood with Billy at the bridge. They had gone to high school together; they'd fished as a team hundreds of times. They never confided in each other, but they had an easygoing way of passing time for long stretches.

Strange, maybe, considering that John Barnard was the only man Billy had ever felt jealous of. Cass liked him too much.

Not that anything had ever happened. But Billy knew she'd get that look in her eyes whenever she was going to see John. Before Christmas parties, Holy Ghost Society Dances, even goddamn PTA meetings. Cass was a flirt, for sure; it only made Billy that much prouder she belonged to him.

Cass and John had dated a couple of times after high school, when Cass had wanted to marry Billy and Billy had been too dumb to ask. Billy, delivering scallops to Lobsterville one night, had met Cass's mother in the kitchen.

"I want to show you something," Mary Keating said. She began leading Billy into the dining room.

"I can't go in there," Billy said, sniffing his sleeve. His rubber boots tracked fragments of scallop shells.

"You'd better, if you don't want to lose her," Mary said. Five-two in her red high heels, Mary Keating had a husky smoker's voice and the drive of a Detroit diesel. Standing in the kitchen doorway, blocking waiters, she pointed across the dining room. There, at a table for two, framed by a picture window overlooking a red sun setting over Mount Hope harbor, were Cass and John having dinner together.

Bonnie and Nora, in their waitress uniforms, hovered nearby.

John was tall, with sandy-brown hair and a movie-hero profile, and the way he and Cass were leaning across the table, smiling into each other's eyes, made Billy want to vault across the bar and smash John's face into his plate. He left without a word, but the incident brought Billy to his senses; two months later, he and Cass were married.

Billy pulled back on the throttle as they passed the No Wake buoy.

"Almost there," John said.

"Can I grab a ride with you?" Billy asked. The Barnards, like most fishing families, lived in Alewives Park.

"Sure," John said. "No problem."

The deck hands checked the dock lines, then stood along the port rail, waiting to jump ashore. Billy threw the engine into reverse, then eased the boat ahead. She bumped hard once, hard again, and then settled into a gentle sway.

In the bestselling tradition of
Amanda Quick, a spectacular new
historical romance from the nationally
bestselling

Jane Feather

"An author to treasure."
—*Romantic Times*

VELVET

Clad in black velvet and posing as a widowed French comtesse, Gabrielle de Beaucaire had returned to England for one purpose only—to ruin the man responsible for her young lover's death. But convincing the forbidding Nathaniel Praed, England's greatest spymaster, that she would make the perfect agent for his secret service would not be easy. And even after Gabrielle had lured the devastatingly attractive lord to her bed, she would have to contend with his distrust—and with the unexpected hunger that his merest touch aroused. . . .

It was a bright clear night, the air crisp, the stars sharp in the limitless black sky. He flung open the window, leaning his elbows on the sill, looking out over the expanse of smooth lawn where frost glittered under the starlight. It would be a beautiful morning for the hunt.

He climbed back into bed and blew out his candle.

He heard the rustling of the woodbine almost immediately. His hand slipped beneath his pillow to his constant companion, the small silver-mounted pistol. He lay very still, every muscle held in waiting, his ears straining into the darkness. The small scratching, rustling sounds continued, drawing closer to the open window. Someone was climbing the thick ancient creeper clinging to the mellow brick walls of the Jacobean manor house.

His hand closed more firmly over the pistol and he hitched himself up on one elbow, his eyes on the square of the window, waiting.

Hands competently gripped the edge of the windowsill, followed by a dark head. The nocturnal visitor swung a leg over the sill and hitched himself upright, straddling the sill.

"Since you've only just snuffed your candle, I'm sure you're still awake," Gabrielle de Beaucaire said into the dark, still room. "And I'm sure you have a pistol, so please don't shoot, it's only me."

Nathaniel was rarely taken by surprise and was a master at concealing it on those rare occasions. On this occasion, however, his training deserted him.

"*Only!*" he exclaimed. "What the hell are you doing?"

"Guess," his visitor challenged cheerfully from her perch.

"You'll have to forgive me, but I don't find guessing games amusing," he declared in clipped accents. He sat up, his pistol still in his hand, and stared at the dark shape outlined against the moonlight. That aura of trouble surrounding Gabrielle de Beaucaire had not been a figment of his imagination.

"Perhaps I should be flattered," he said icily. "Am I to assume unbridled lust lies behind the honor of this visit, madam?" His eyes narrowed.

Disconcertingly, the woman appeared to be impervious to irony. She laughed. A warm, merry sound that Nathaniel found as incongruous in the circumstances as it was disturbingly attractive.

"Not at his point, Lord Praed; but there's no saying what the future might hold." It was a mischievous and outrageous statement that rendered him temporarily speechless.

She took something out of the pocket of her britches and held it on the palm of her hand. "I'm here to present my credentials."

She swung off the windowsill and approached the bed, a sinuous figure in her black britches and glimmering white shirt.

He leaned sideways, struck flint on tinder, and relit the bedside candle. The dark red hair glowed in the light as she extended her hand, palm upward, toward him and he saw what she held.

It was a small scrap of black velvet cut with a ragged edge.

"Well, well." The evening's puzzles were finally solved. Lord Praed opened a drawer in the bedside table and took out a piece of tissue paper. Unfolding it, he revealed the twin of the scrap of material.

"I should have guessed," he said pensively. "Only a woman would have come up with such a fanciful idea." He took the velvet from her extended palm and fitted the ragged edge to the other piece, making a whole square. "So you're Simon's surprise. No wonder he was so secretive. But what makes you think I would ever employ a woman?"

WITCH DANCE

BY

Peggy Webb

"Ms. Webb has an inventive mind brimming with originality that makes all of her books special reading."—*Romantic Times*

An exquisite woman of ivory and jade, she'd come to Witch Dance, Oklahoma, to bring modern medicine to the native Chickasaw people. But when Dr. Kate Malone saw the magnificent Indian rising from the river, naked as sin and twice as tempting, every thought of duty was lost, drowned in a primitive wave of longing that made her tremble with desire. . . .

He was more man than she'd ever seen. And every gorgeous inch of him was within touching distance.

For all he seemed to care, he could have been bending over her in a Brooks Brothers suit.

"What impulse sent you into the river?" He squatted beside her with both hands on her shoulders, and she'd never felt skin as hot in her life.

" I thought you were drowning."

His laughter was deep and melodious, and as sensual as exotic music played in some dark corner of a dimly lit café where lovers embraced.

"I am Chickasaw," he said, as if that explained everything.

"Well, I'm human and I made a mistake." She pushed her wet hair away from her face. "Why can't you just admit you made a mistake, staying under the water so long I thought you were going to drown?"

"You were watching me?"

"No . . . yes . . ." His legs were powerful, heavily muscled, bent in such a way that the best parts of him were hidden. He leaned closer, intent on answers. How did he expect her to think straight with his leg touching hers like that? "Not deliberately," she said. "I was on a picnic. How did I know you'd be cavorting about in the river without any clothes on?"

He searched her face with eyes deep and black. Then he touched her cheeks, his strong hands exquisitely gentle.

"I'm sorry I ruined your picnic." Ever so tenderly his hands roamed over her face. Breathless, she sat beside the river, his willing captive. "You've scratched your face . . . here . . . and here."

Until that moment she hadn't known that every nerve in the body could tremble. Now she could attest to it as a medical fact.

". . . and your legs." He gave her legs the same tender attention he'd given her face. She would have sold her soul to feel his hands on her forever. "I have remedies for your injuries."

Oh, God. Would he kiss them and make them well? She almost said it.

"I can fix them . . ." How? She could barely breathe. "I'm a doctor."

"You came to Tribal Lands to practice medicine?"

"You doubt my word?"

"No. Your commitment."

"Is it because I'm white that you think I'm not committed, or because I'm female?"

"Neither, *Wictonaye*." In one fluid movement he stood before her, smiling.

And in that moment her world changed. Colors

and light receded, faded, until there was nothing except the bold Chickasaw with his glowing, polished skin and his seductive voice that obliterated every thought, every need except the most basic . . . to die of love. Sitting on the hard ground, looking up at her nameless captor, she wanted to die in the throes of passion.

She stood on shaky, uncertain legs. Clenching her fists by her side, she faced him.

"If you're going to call me names, use English, please."

"*Wictonaye* . . . wildcat."

"I've been called worse." Would God forgive her if she left right now? Would He give her the healing touch and allow her to save lives if she forgot about her lust and focused on her mission?

She spun around, then felt his hand on her arm.

"I've been rude. It's not my way."

"Nor mine." She grinned. "Except sometimes."

"You tried to save my life, and I don't know your name."

"Kate Malone."

"Thank you for saving my life, Kate Malone." His eyes sparkled with wicked glee. She'd never known a man of such boldness . . . nor such appeal. "I'm Eagle Mingo."

"Next time you decide to play in the river, Eagle Mingo, be more careful. I might not be around to rescue you."

She marched toward the bluff, thinking it was a good exit, until he appeared beside her, still naked as sin and twice as tempting.

"You forgot your shoe." He held out one of her moccasins.

"Thanks." Lord, did he expect her to bend down

and put it on with him standing there like that? She hobbled along, half shoeless.

"And your picnic basket." He scooped it off the ground and handed it to her. Then, damned if he didn't bow like some courtly knight in shining armor.

If she ever got home, she'd have to take an aspirin and go to bed. Doctor's orders.

"Good-bye. Enjoy your"—her eyes raked him from head to toe, and she could feel her whole body getting hot—"swim."

She didn't know how she got up the bluff, but she didn't draw a good breath until she was safely at the top. He was still standing down there, looking up. She could feel his eyes on her.

Lest he think she was a total coward, she put on her other shoe, then turned and casually waved at him. At least she hoped it was casual.

Dammit all, he waved back. Facing full front. She might never recover.

And don't miss these incredible romances from Bantam Books, on sale in August:

THE LAST
BACHELOR
by the nationally bestselling author

Betina Krahn

"One of the genre's most creative writers."
—*Romantic Times*

PRINCE OF
WOLVES
by the sensational

Susan Krinard

A romance of mystery, magic, and forbidden passion

WHISPERED LIES
by the highly acclaimed

Christy Cohen
A novel of dangerous desires and seductive secrets

OFFICIAL RULES

To enter the sweepstakes below carefully follow all instructions found elsewhere in this offer.

The **Winners Classic** will award prizes with the following approximate maximum values: 1 Grand Prize: $26,500 (or $25,000 cash alternate); 1 First Prize: $3,000; 5 Second Prizes: $400 each; 35 Third Prizes: $100 each; 1,000 Fourth Prizes: $7.50 each. Total maximum retail value of Winners Classic Sweepstakes is $42,500. Some presentations of this sweepstakes may contain individual entry numbers corresponding to one or more of the aforementioned prize levels. To determine the Winners, individual entry numbers will first be compared with the winning numbers preselected by computer. For winning numbers not returned, prizes will be awarded in random drawings from among all eligible entries received. Prize choices may be offered at various levels. If a winner chooses an automobile prize, all license and registration fees, taxes, destination charges and, other expenses not offered herein are the responsibility of the winner. If a winner chooses a trip, travel must be complete within one year from the time the prize is awarded. Minors must be accompanied by an adult. Travel companion(s) must also sign release of liability. Trips are subject to space and departure availability. Certain black-out dates may apply.

The following applies to the sweepstakes named above:

No purchase necessary. You can also enter the sweepstakes by sending your name and address to: P.O. Box 508, Gibbstown, N.J. 08027. Mail each entry separately. Sweepstakes begins 6/1/93. Entries must be received by 12/30/94. Not responsible for lost, late, damaged, misdirected, illegible or postage due mail. Mechanically reproduced entries are not eligible. All entries become property of the sponsor and will not be returned.

Prize Selection/Validations: Selection of winners will be conducted no later than 5:00 PM on January 28, 1995, by an independent judging organization whose decisions are final. Random drawings will be held at 1211 Avenue of the Americas, New York, N.Y. 10036. Entrants need not be present to win. Odds of winning are determined by total number of entries received. Circulation of this sweepstakes is estimated not to exceed 200 million. All prizes are guaranteed to be awarded and delivered to winners. Winners will be notified by mail and may be required to complete an affidavit of eligibility and release of liability which must be returned within 14 days of date on notification or alternate winners will be selected in a random drawing. Any prize notification letter or any prize returned to a participating sponsor, Bantam Doubleday Dell Publishing Group, Inc., its participating divisions or subsidiaries, or the independent judging organization as undeliverable will be awarded to an alternate winner. Prizes are not transferable. No substitution for prizes except as offered or as may be necessary due to unavailability, in which case a prize of equal or greater value will be awarded. Prizes will be awarded approximately 90 days after the drawing. All taxes are the sole responsibility of the winners. Entry constitutes permission (except where prohibited by law) to use winners' names, hometowns, and likenesses for publicity purposes without further or other compensation. Prizes won by minors will be awarded in the name of parent or legal guardian.

Participation: Sweepstakes open to residents of the United States and Canada, except for the province of Quebec. Sweepstakes sponsored by Bantam Doubleday Dell Publishing Group, Inc., (BDD), 1540 Broadway, New York, NY 10036. Versions of this sweepstakes with different graphics and prize choices will be offered in conjunction with various solicitations or promotions by different subsidiaries and divisions of BDD. Where applicable, winners will have their choice of any prize offered at level won. Employees of BDD, its divisions, subsidiaries, advertising agencies, independent judging organization, and their immediate family members are not eligible.

Canadian residents, in order to win, must first correctly answer a time limited arithmetical skill testing question. Void in Puerto Rico, Quebec and wherever prohibited or restricted by law. Subject to all federal, state, local and provincial laws and regulations. For a list of major prize winners (available after 1/29/95): send a self-addressed, stamped envelope entirely separate from your entry to: Sweepstakes Winners, P.O. Box 517, Gibbstown, NJ 08027. Requests must be received by 12/30/94. DO NOT SEND ANY OTHER CORRESPONDENCE TO THIS P.O. BOX.

Bestselling Women's Fiction

Sandra Brown

28951-9	TEXAS! LUCKY	$5.99/6.99 in Canada
28990-X	TEXAS! CHASE	$5.99/6.99
29500-4	TEXAS! SAGE	$5.99/6.99
29085-1	22 INDIGO PLACE	$5.99/6.99
29783-X	A WHOLE NEW LIGHT	$5.99/6.99
56045-X	TEMPERATURES RISING	$5.99/6.99
56274-6	FANTA C	$4.99/5.99
56278-9	LONG TIME COMING	$4.99/5.99

Amanda Quick

28354-5	SEDUCTION	$5.99/6.99
28932-2	SCANDAL	$5.99/6.99
28594-7	SURRENDER	$5.99/6.99
29325-7	RENDEZVOUS	$5.99/6.99
29316-8	RECKLESS	$5.99/6.99
29316-8	RAVISHED	$4.99/5.99
29317-6	DANGEROUS	$5.99/6.99
56506-0	DECEPTION	$5.99/7.50

Nora Roberts

29078-9	GENUINE LIES	$5.99/6.99
28578-5	PUBLIC SECRETS	$5.99/6.99
26461-3	HOT ICE	$5.99/6.99
26574-1	SACRED SINS	$5.99/6.99
27859-2	SWEET REVENGE	$5.99/6.99
27283-7	BRAZEN VIRTUE	$5.99/6.99
29597-7	CARNAL INNOCENCE	$5.50/6.50
29490-3	DIVINE EVIL	$5.99/6.99

Iris Johansen

29871-2	LAST BRIDGE HOME	$4.50/5.50
29604-3	THE GOLDEN BARBARIAN	$4.99/5.99
29244-7	REAP THE WIND	$4.99/5.99
29032-0	STORM WINDS	$4.99/5.99
28855-5	THE WIND DANCER	$4.95/5.95
29968-9	THE TIGER PRINCE	$5.50/6.50
29944-1	THE MAGNIFICENT ROGUE	$5.99/6.99
29945-X	BELOVED SCOUNDREL	$5.99/6.99

Ask for these titles at your bookstore or use this page to order.